Faith, Rope, and Love

FAITH AND FOILS
COZY MYSTERY SERIES #4

WENDY HEUVEL

OLDE
CROW
PUBLISHING

Faith, Rope, and Love
Faith and Foils Cozy Mystery Series – Book 4

Published in Ontario, Canada by Olde Crow Publishing.

Cover design by http://www.StunningBookCovers.com

Publisher's Note: This novel is a work of fiction. Names, characters, places, and incidents are either products of the author's imagination or used fictitiously. All characters are fictional, and any similarity to people living or dead is purely coincidental.

ISBN: 978-1-990081-03-3 (paperback edition)
ISBN: 978-1-990081-04-0 (hardcover edition)
ISBN: 978-1-990081-02-6 (e-book)

Faith, Rope, and Love

Chapter 1

Cassie Bridgestone tightened the collar of her winter coat as an icy February breeze whipped by and lifted a dusting of snow from the sidewalk. She tried to dodge the swirling snow, but it hit her square in the face, also sprinkling her friends Lexy and Daniel.

"Pfft!" Cassie wiped her face with her mitten and brushed off the blonde curls beneath her hat.

Lexy shook the snow from her own toque. "Maybe we should have taken the SUV."

"Really, you two?" Daniel laughed, his blue eyes shining. "It's only a couple of blocks. Besides, we're Canadians."

Cassie narrowed her eyes and swiped her hand across the top of the tall snowbank lining the sidewalk. By the time she packed a nice snowball into her palm,

Daniel was about ten steps ahead. She chucked the snowball and hit him square in the back.

"Hey! Watch the present!" He turned and held up the large gift bag in front of his face.

Lexy giggled. "Shame on you, using a baby's gift for cover."

"I have no shame."

Cassie whipped another snowball and laughed as it connected with Daniel's shoulder. She brushed her hands together to wipe the snow off her mittens and caught up with the others.

Despite the weather being below freezing, it was a beautiful Saturday afternoon. Sunlight extended from the grey sky to kiss the snow-covered village of Banford. Smoke rose from the chimneys of the old stone homes, and chickadees flitted from bush to bush, shaking snow off the branches as they landed. A bright red cardinal stood out against the white backdrop as it landed on a birdfeeder swinging from an old maple tree.

Cassie returned the wave of a man shovelling his driveway and took a couple of steps back to watch Lexy and Daniel. Lexy had been Cassie's best friend for years. She was kinder and more loyal than anyone you could ever meet.

And Daniel, well—he was Daniel Sawyer. The handsome, well-built, big-city photographer turned bookstore owner and her tenant. His rugged jawline and solid muscles made her head spin, and his compassionate and loving personality made her heart spin. Being with him felt like coming home after a hard day of work. Yet, although he now shared Cassie's faith in God, and she was sure his feelings for her had grown beyond friendship, she still held off from pursuing a romantic relationship with him.

Her heart was tempted, but her mind held her back. She'd learned her lesson after rushing into dating the kind and loving Spencer. His near perfection had clouded her judgement. In the end, he'd been all wrong for her, and she'd had to break it off after a couple of months. Even though it had happened before Christmas, she was still trying to forgive herself for wounding Spencer. There was no way she could also risk hurting Daniel too.

"Are you coming?" Lexy turned around to wait for Cassie. Her puffy white coat, hat and mitts made her blend into the snowbank behind her.

"Sorry. Just daydreaming."

Daniel hunched his shoulders and shivered. "It's too cold for that. Hurry up!"

"I thought you were Canadian?"

"I am. But I'm not a narwhal."

Lexy snorted. "A what?"

"A narwhal. Whale species in the north that thrives in cold waters? The one with the unicorn horn."

Cassie laughed so hard she nearly tripped. "Really? Of all the arctic species to compare yourself to, *that's* the first one to pop in your mind?"

"What would you have said?"

"I dunno. Arctic fox?"

Daniel lifted his chin and smirked. "Huh. You think I'm a fox, do you?"

Cassie threw another snowball in Daniel's direction and skipped ahead, hoping he wouldn't see her face, which was a nice shade of pink by the feeling of it. Daniel *was* a fox. Why couldn't she have said polar bear? "Fine. How about a willow ptarmigan?"

Lexy shook her head. "Let me guess. That's a bird?"

"Of course. They're really cool! In the summer, they're brown, with a red spot above their eye. But in the winter, their plumage turns white, so they blend into the snow. Their feet are full of feathers to help them walk on the snow, but they also dig out burrows to keep—"

"Oh, look! Anna's street!" Lexy grinned and pointed.

Cassie pursed her lips together in a mock pout. "Fine. I'll tell Anna about the ptarmigan. She'll listen!" She marched ahead to feign annoyance.

"I was listening," Daniel called after her. "Really!"

Cassie giggled. Anna had first become Cassie's friend through the Banford Bird Club. Their shared love of birds had instantly bonded them, and they had grown even closer since Cassie had helped clear Anna's boyfriend, Zach, of a murder charge last summer.

Cassie, Daniel, and Lexy approached a small yellow bungalow with tips of a white picket fence peeking out above the snow. Anna and Zach had just purchased the cute little home in Banford, only a few weeks before their first baby was due to arrive.

Lexy and Cassie had put a housewarming gift bag together with a blanket, wall stickers, picture frames, and a mobile for the baby's room. Daniel came along to help Zach assemble the crib.

They walked up the freshly shovelled walk, and Daniel knocked on the door.

A very pregnant Anna let them in. "Hi! You made it!"

Cassie had to step to the side to get around Anna's belly. "Hi! Where's Zach? You shouldn't be answering the door. It's too cold outside. And you should be resting!"

Anna laughed and squeezed the door shut behind the group. "I'm pregnant, not sick." But you aren't kidding about the cold." She rubbed her hands together and shivered.

"Hey, guys!" Zach appeared in the hallway, scratching his beard.

"This place is charming," Lexy said.

"Thanks. We really like it."

"I'm so glad you finally found a place you both loved." Cassie shook her hat out above the doormat.

Anna leaned against Zach. "Me too. Do you want a tour?"

"We'd love one." Cassie hung her coat on a hook over Lexy's and grabbed the gift bag from Daniel.

Anna led them through a doorway. "This is the

living room." Two blue fabric loveseats sat against the walls, while a cozy area rug added warmth to the hardwood floors, while a few unpacked boxes sat in the corner. A large picture window offered a grand view of the cute yard and the street.

"This is so nice!" Cassie set the gift bag on the floor and looked out over the yard.

"It's the perfect place to raise our family. And on a nice quiet street, too."

"Except for the haunted house across the way." Lexy pointed out the window.

Zach laughed. "Yeah. I've heard those stories."

"What stories?" Anna rubbed her belly.

"Nothing to worry about, Hon. It's just an empty house."

Daniel stepped up to the window. "Which house?"

"Ha! You didn't notice when we walked by? Where was your focus?" Lexy glanced at Cassie. "As if we didn't know."

Cassie ignored Lexy's comment and pointed the house out to Daniel.

His mouth fell agape. "Wow! Look at that place!" The abandoned, two-storey mansion stood across the street from Zach and Anna's bungalow. The windows were mostly boarded up, and the roof had missing shingles and even a few holes.

"I know." Cassie smiled. "Isn't it beautiful?"

"That's not a word I would've chosen." He furrowed his brows.

"Me either," Lexy added. "The place should be torn down."

"I agree," Daniel said.

"No!" Cassie put her hand on Daniel's arm. "It has such… charm. Look at the turret. And the covered porch! There's even a little dormer for a tiny room in the attic."

"You've been in there before?"

"No, but I've imagined what it must be like since I was a kid."

Lexy frowned. "I imagine it's full of cobwebs and mice."

"But think of what it must have been like in its glory days." Cassie sighed.

"I bet it was nice. Before the ghost showed up." Lexy looked at pale-faced Anna. "I'm teasing. There's definitely nothing to worry about."

"Quiet neighbours, anyway." Daniel grinned. "Ready to tackle the crib, Zach?"

"For sure." Zach sighed in relief. "I'm about to pull my hair out over that thing." He led Daniel down the hall.

"Ugh." Anna put her hand on her back and sighed. "This baby weighs a ton!"

"Well, have a seat then." Cassie rushed to Anna's side and urged her to sit. She put a cushion behind Anna's back to help her friend get comfortable and sat beside her. "We can get the tour some other time."

"Yes." Lexy grabbed the gift bag and brought it to

Anna. "You can open this instead."

"Oh, you guys! You're so sweet. But I'll wait for Zach." She set the bag on the floor beside her feet.

Cassie patted Anna's leg. "How are you feeling? Other than your back?"

"Yes." Lexy sat on the opposite sofa. "Moving this close to your due date must really be increasing your stress."

"It's not too bad. Zach's been doing almost everything. If you're going to feel bad for someone, feel bad for him."

"Are you still sending him to Drummond's Bakery every day for the cinnamon rolls?" Cassie giggled.

"Not every day, but yes. I thought cravings were supposed to subside in the third trimester, but so far, they haven't."

"At least you have a good excuse." Lexy turned to Cassie and smirked.

"What's that supposed to mean?" Cassie fluttered her eyelashes, pretending to take offence. "Besides, it's doughnuts for me. Not cinnamon rolls. Although they can be good too…"

The girls laughed.

"Where's Caramel?" Cassie asked, suddenly remembering Anna's cute, brown tabby.

"Still hiding. I think he's under the bed today."

"He'll get used to it. Give him time."

"I'm not so sure. I'm kind of worried. Any other time I've moved, he's come out pretty quickly. He's usually not so shy."

"Maybe he knows the baby's coming?" Lexy asked. "Do cats get jealous?"

Cassie chewed the inside of her cheek. "Maybe. If he doesn't come out soon, I can bring Pumpkin by." She smiled at the thought of her big orange-and-white kitty. "They get along so well, maybe Pumpkin can coax him to come out? She's used to going places and seeing strangers—like at the shop. It won't bother her to come here."

"I'll keep it in mind. Thanks." Anna placed a hand on Cassie's arm. "And speaking of the shop, who's handling it today?"

"Grams and Maggie. They insisted I have a Saturday off." Cassie thought of her dear grandmother and sister-in-law. She was so blessed to have them work with her at her country store, Olde Crow Primitives. Grams used to own the store, but Cassie bought the building from her a few years ago. Now Grams stayed on to work without having to do all the fussy bookkeeping stuff, as she called it. And Maggie worked part-time, coming in when she wasn't helping her husband Rick, Cassie's brother, with his real estate business.

"That was nice of them." Anna placed her hands on her belly. "What else do you plan to do today? Are you going to look for the eagles?"

Cassie's face lit up. "Most definitely. I'm going to head over there after our visit."

"I saw one fly overhead the other day. It was a—"

"And here we go." Lexy feigned a yawn.

"Oh, come on, Lex. Even you would be in awe of their death spiral," Cassie said.

"Death spiral?"

"It's part of their mating ritual. It's one of the most coveted things to see in the birding world."

"Not only in the birding world," Anna added.

"Okay." Lexy rolled her head back. "I give in. Tell me all about it."

Cassie sat forward on the sofa. "It's amazing! The male and female meet high, high up in the sky and lock talons. Then they plummet to the earth while spinning around in cartwheels. They hang on until they're almost at the ground."

"That does sound cool."

"It's spectacular."

"How many times have you seen it?"

Cassie sat back and frowned. "Never. That's why I'm so determined this year. There's nothing I'd rather see more."

"Oh, really?" Lexy grinned as the boys returned to the room.

Cassie willed her face to stop heating up, but it refused.

"Say, what now?" Daniel asked.

"They're talking about birds again." Lexy crossed her legs. "Eagles this time. And some sort of death spiral."

Zach sighed. "I've heard all about it."

"Oh, stop." Anna waved her hand at him. He chuckled.

"Crib all together?" Cassie asked.

"No." Daniel rubbed the back of his neck. "We're going to give it another try tomorrow. I need to grab some tools from my place."

"Yeah," Zach nodded. "I'm not sure which box mine are in."

"What kind of tools do you need to put a crib together?" Lexy furrowed her brows.

"Hammer, drill, maybe a saw."

"What?" Cassie laughed. "I'm pretty sure you don't need a saw."

"You wanna try? Come look at the crib of a million parts."

"No, no. I'm good. It's time to get going to the river anyway. I want to check for the eagles."

"Let's all head out then." Lexy stood. "Anna probably needs some rest."

"Sounds good. See you tomorrow?" Daniel asked.

Zach nodded. "Sure."

"Now we have a few minutes to check out the mansion before we head back." Daniel rubbed his hands together.

"What?" Cassie's eyes opened wide.

"I want to take a peek. Aren't you curious?"

"Well, yeah. But—"

"Where's your sense of adventure?"

"Don't tempt her." Lexy laughed.

11

Cassie frowned. "I'm not sure it's a good idea."

"C'mon." Daniel winked. "Don't be a chicken."

"I'm not chicken. I just don't want to disturb it."

"A little late for that." Lexy raised her brows. "That house has been disturbing for a long time."

"Very funny. You know what I mean."

Daniel shrugged. "Well, I'm heading over. Come if you want."

"I'm in!" Lexy beamed.

"Fine." Cassie dropped her shoulders. "But only to make sure you don't wreck anything."

"Be careful," Anna warned.

Zach grinned. "And watch out for the ghosts."

Chapter 2

Daniel pulled his gloves tighter onto his hands and crossed the street.

"Wait! What are you going to do? Break in?" Cassie tromped after him and met him on the sidewalk in front of the derelict mansion.

"Well, I doubt the front door's unlocked."

"But I don't want you to damage anything." She looped her arm through his.

Lexy stepped up behind them. "Are you looking at the same place I'm looking at?"

"I just mean I don't want anyone to cause *more* damage."

"Come on." Daniel stepped into the deep snow

where it appeared the walkway should be. "Let's get closer."

Cassie carefully stepped into the boot tracks left by Daniel and followed him onto the front porch. Snow had blown in and covered half the porch and decorated the remains of a couple of broken-down wicker chairs.

"Can't you see it?" Cassie whirled around. "I bet flowered pots hung from those metal hangers. And surely those hooks held a porch swing."

Lexy and Daniel exchanged glances.

"What?"

Daniel laughed. "I see broken soffit, loose deck boards, and a cracked post that's about to make the porch roof collapse under the weight of the snow."

"Such a romantic." Cassie put her hand on her hip.

Lexy approached the front entry. The outer, wooden screen door hung on an angle from only one hinge at the top. She tugged on it, but it didn't budge. "I think it's frozen."

"Let me try." Daniel grabbed the door on both sides and gave it a tug. The remaining hinge let go, leaving him standing holding the entire door in the air. "Uh. There?"

Lexy laughed. "Whatever works!"

"Please be careful," Cassie pleaded as she helped Daniel set the door against the wall.

Lexy tugged and pushed on the old brass handle. "Door's locked."

"Too bad." Cassie shrugged. "Let's go then."

"Nice try." Daniel tried the door handle himself, then backed up and examined the front of the house. "Maybe there's an open window or a loose panel."

Cassie frowned and crossed her arms as Lexy and Daniel parted ways walking opposite directions on the porch, following it around the sides of the house to check for any openings.

Daniel soon reappeared around the corner. "Here!" He waved her over. "I think I found a way."

Cassie sighed and waited for Lexy, who quickly returned from her side. Together they carefully picked their way along the porch, avoiding snowdrifts and broken boards. As they rounded the corner, Daniel had already removed a large piece of weathered plywood from in front of a window opening.

"See?" He set the wood down. "That one was only held up by a couple of old nails."

"And how are you going to put it back up when we're done?" Cassie stared at him.

"I'll pop over tomorrow with my hammer on my way to Zach's. Okay?"

"Okay."

Daniel raised his leg over the windowsill. Within seconds, he disappeared inside the house. A hand popped out towards Cassie. "M'lady?"

"Lexy. You're next." Cassie crossed her arms again.

"I'm pretty sure he meant you."

"Fine." Cassie unfolded her arms and grabbed Daniel's hand. Even through her mittens, she could feel the electricity from his touch.

"Be careful." He gently grabbed her arm. "There's still some broken glass stuck to the frame."

Cassie let him lead her into the house. As her feet hit the worn, dusty floor, she stomped them to remove any loose snow—no sense traipsing it through the house.

Lexy hopped through the window and appeared beside her. She looked up. "Woah."

Cassie followed Lexy's gaze. Faint light broke through the few remaining windows and the opening they just came through. The sight was nothing like Cassie had expected.

They stood in a grand room, with high ceilings and an old wooden staircase leading to the second floor. The handrail curved at the bottom with a touch of elegance. An old chandelier still hung from the ceiling, the remaining crystal droplets catching the odd hint of light between all the cobwebs and dust hanging from them.

But most unusual of all, the room remained full of furniture and old belongings. An old chaise lounge stood against the far wall, with a dust layer almost as thick as the pillows on it. Paintings hung, their pictures barely decipherable between the darkness and the coat of grime covering them. Graffiti names in spray paint covered the blank areas on the wall. A desk full of yellowed papers and warped books stood in one corner—an old grand piano in the other.

Cassie's mouth hung agape as she took in the sights around her. "It's… it's…"

"Like a museum," Daniel said.

"Someone just walked away from everything." Lexy shook her head. "It's hard to believe."

Daniel stepped over a loose floorboard and grabbed a framed photo from a small table by the staircase. He blew on the picture, and while some dust blew off, a thick layer of dirt remained. He rubbed the glass with the thumb of his glove to clear a spot.

"What is it?" Cassie peered over his shoulder.

"Looks like a photo of a woman." As he cleared more glass and held the photo up to the light, the faint image of a lady appeared. She wore a sixties-style mini dress with what must have been psychedelic flowers before the picture had faded. Her long hair was held off her forehead by a thick hairband, and the ends bounced off her shoulder with a flip.

"I bet she's the ghost." Lexy jabbed the photo with her forefinger.

"Would you stop with that?" Cassie said.

"Tell me more about this ghost." Daniel returned the photo to the table.

"Rumour has it the married couple who lived here in the sixties had a big fight, and they both ran off. Years later, after she died, her ghost returned to protect the house while she waited for his ghost to join her here."

"Whatever." Cassie rolled her eyes.

"I would think that would add to your romantic

notion about the place." Daniel gently grabbed her arm.

She ignored the sparks from his touch. "It would, except ghosts aren't real. At least not those kinds."

"There are kinds that are?" Lexy asked.

"Well, no. I mean—you know what I mean. There are angels and demons in the spiritual realm, but the whole I'm-haunting-you-after-I-die thing isn't real." She made air quotes with her fingers, forgetting they were covered by mittens. "Oh. Those were air quotes…"

Daniel laughed. "I guessed."

"Obviously, I don't believe it's haunted either," Lexy said. "But that's the story."

Daniel stepped farther into the room. "But *something* strange happened here. Who would just up and walk away from their house?"

"Maybe the first part of Lexy's story is true. Maybe there really was an argument, and both the husband and the wife left."

"It's not *my* story. But it does make sense. What other explanation could there be?"

Daniel made his way over to the grand piano and pressed a key. The hammer moved but only struck a mat of dust. Even so, a very faint hum from the string vibrated through the room. "Do you think they both left, not knowing the other also walked away?"

Cassie shook her head. "That's silly. It still doesn't make sense. Even if you were going to walk away from a marriage, you'd take your things with you, wouldn't you?"

"Maybe they packed a suitcase." Lexy shrugged. "Let's check out the rest of the house."

"Hey!" The room dimmed as a figure blocked light from the window they'd just entered. An old man stared at them, the ear flaps of his plaid woollen hat sticking out at the sides. His nose was big and red, and his eyes were too tiny for the rest of his face. "Get out of here before I call the cops!"

Lexy shimmied behind Cassie to hide. In part, she *was* 'the cops'. She was the administrative assistant for the Ontario Provincial Police satellite office in Banford and worked for the local officer, Brent.

"We're sorry!" Cassie held her hands up out of instinct. "We mean no harm." She nudged Daniel on her way by.

"Don't care. You don't belong here, so scram!"

Cassie gingerly approached the man who stood on the opposite side of the window. "Do you live near here? Our friends just moved across the street."

"Them? Figures. Only takes one young couple to bring all kinds of riffraff into the neighbourhood."

"No, no. They're quite kind! They're expecting a baby soon."

"Great. I was hoping she was just fat." The man snorted. "That's all we need around here. A screaming kid."

"You're not very nice! I'll have you know—"

"We'll be leaving right away, Sir." Daniel grabbed

19

Cassie's arm and gently pulled her away from the window. "So sorry to disturb you. No need to call the cops."

"And make sure you hang that board back up!" He sneered.

"I'll be bringing a hammer by tomorrow to take care of it properly."

"Whatever." The man waved his hand and stomped across the snowy porch, as much as his old, feeble legs would let him. "Dumb riffraff. Gotta cause problems on my street..." He continued to mutter as he disappeared around the corner.

Lexy placed her hand on Cassie's arm. "Did you really say, 'We mean no harm?' Did you think he was an alien or something?"

"Very funny."

Daniel laughed. "He did kind of look like one with that hat."

Lexy giggled. "Well, let's go." She climbed out of the window. "Brent would kill me if he answered a call and I was the culprit."

"I *told* you we shouldn't have come here." Cassie allowed Daniel to help her through the window.

"But aren't you glad you got to peek inside?" He hopped out after her.

"That's not the point, is it?"

"Ha! I knew it."

A satisfying glint settled in his eyes, causing a warmth to spread through Cassie's chest. Had he done this for her? Knowing she'd longed to see the inside? Cassie playfully swatted his arm as they left the porch and followed their footsteps back out to the sidewalk.

Daniel was right. She'd avoided the house her whole life, fearing reality would burst the romantic image she'd created over the years. How wrong she'd been. A glimpse into the young couple's long-forgotten life was better than she'd dreamed.

Way better.

Not only did the grand home surpass her dreams, but the place also came with a mystery. She couldn't wait to get home and research the history.

But first, it was time to look for the eagles and a little romance in the skies.

Chapter 3

Cassie lifted her backpack onto the kitchen table and checked the contents one more time. Binoculars? Check. Scope? Check. Bird books? Check. Collapsible tripod? Snacks? Water? Check, check, check.

"Rowr?" Pumpkin, Cassie's large orange-and-white tabby, jumped on the table.

"Hey! Get down, you!" Cassie gave the cat a shove, but instead of pushing her off the table, she only succeeded in mashing the cat's fat rolls together.

"Rowr!" Pumpkin stood her ground.

"Fine. I'll give you some attention." Cassie smiled and used both arms to pick up the cat and cradled her like a baby. "Who's my favourite kitty? Who's my baby bear?" She nuzzled the cat and enjoyed the feel of the soft fur against her cheek.

A knock on the apartment door distracted her. "Come in!" She set the cat on the floor.

Daniel appeared, with a backpack of his own. "Hi! Thanks for letting me tag along."

"Of course! The more, the merrier. Eagles are for everyone to enjoy."

"Hey, Pumpkin!" Daniel crouched as the cat waddled over to him. "How's baby bear today?"

Cassie felt heat rise to her cheeks. "Oh. You heard that?"

"No worries. I'm sure anyone would be happy to be your baby bear."

Cassie cocked an eyebrow.

"I mean any cat, or dog, any… animal. Not…" He ran his hand over the back of his neck as his face grew red. "Are you ready to go?"

Cassie giggled. "Sure."

He waited as she put on her snow pants, boots, coat, hat, mitts and scarf. "Are you ready to go, *now?*" He glanced at his watch.

"Very funny."

"Not trying to be funny. But I could've run across the street to get a coffee in the meantime…"

Cassie playfully swatted his arm and grabbed her backpack. "I'll be back soon, baby bear!" She smirked as she patted Pumpkin on the head before closing the door on her way out.

Daniel followed Cassie down the stairs, out onto the street, and across the park to the Rideau River. She turned to follow a trail along the shore, grateful people had already been using it since the last snowfall, so she didn't have to trudge through deep snow and make the trail herself.

As they made their way along the river, between snow-covered shrubs and branches coated in white, a few chickadees called to one another and flitted from bush to bush, following along. Cassie felt a twinge of guilt as she recalled going down this same path last fall with Spencer to have a picnic under the big tree at the end. Was it wrong to be here with Daniel, now? Was she treating him like a cheap substitute?

But then again, they weren't seeing each other, so why would it be wrong?

Maybe she shouldn't have invited Daniel. Would it give him the wrong idea? No, he knew she just wanted to be friends. But if it was okay to be here with him, why was her stomach turning over?

"What's that?" Daniel pointed to a bird landing in a large tree ahead.

Thankful for the distraction, Cassie stopped and whipped her backpack off her shoulder, ready to get her binoculars out. As the bag hit the ground, she stopped. "It's only a crow." She threw the bag back on.

"How can you tell from here? How do you know it's not a raven?"

"Easy. Size, shape, mannerisms. Not to mention

sound. Do you hear him calling?"

Daniel turned his ear toward the tree. "Oh. Yeah."

"And see how he stretches out his neck and rocks when he caws?"

"Yeah. The bounces match the calls."

"Exactly. Ravens don't do that. They only hunch their wings a little. Not to mention they're bigger than crows, and their bills are thicker. When you see the same birds over and over again, you get to know them. You start recognizing them by what they do as much as by what they look like. Kind of the same way you recognize people you know from a distance."

Daniel turned his eyes to Cassie and stared at her with a smile. The sunlight bounced off the snow, making his blue eyes sparkle.

"What?"

"You're so passionate when you speak about birds. It's very cute."

"Cute?" Cassie continued on the trail, walking ahead of Daniel, so she didn't have to see his face—and so he couldn't see hers as he talked about her.

"Cute might not be the right word. Beautiful, maybe?"

"Maybe?" Cassie laughed.

"Definitely."

She swallowed and continued walking. She didn't mean for this to turn into an opportunity for him to compliment her in that way. While it caused a warmth to flow through her, it also caused confusion. Her brain fought against her heart, and the resulting turmoil made her feel nauseous. Spencer's face swam into her mind's eye. She'd hurt him. She'd rushed ahead of God, and the results were disastrous. She couldn't do that to Daniel, too. She wouldn't.

"There's the blind." Cassie lifted her pack off her shoulder again as they approached a dilapidated wooden lean-to standing on the shore. The roof carried the weight of the last snowfall, but the constant, chilly wind picked away at it, sending tufts of snow into the air. Surrounding the blind, bent, brown reeds of last year's cattails peeked out from the snow. Cassie tightened the scarf around her neck to cut off the piercing wind as she stepped into the blind and sat on the bench.

Daniel plopped down beside her. "Whew! Who knew it would be so much colder out here?" His breath became visible in the freezing air.

"Me. That's why I wore all this winter stuff."

"Hey. I'm prepared!" He held up his hands covered in large ski mitts.

"And I'm even more prepared." Cassie unzipped her backpack and pulled out two thermoses. "Hot chocolate?"

"Ah! Yes! And yours is Earl Grey tea, I presume?"

"Nothing but!"

They opened their thermoses and sipped their hot drinks, the steam creating a bit of a cloud between them.

After a few sips, Cassie replaced the lid on the

thermos and yanked her binoculars out. She removed the case and lens cap, leaving them ready on the bench beside her. Then she pulled out the tripod, extended the legs, and mounted the scope on top.

"Quite the setup! Want to see mine?" Daniel pulled out binoculars of his own.

"Hey! When did you get those?"

"A couple of weeks ago. I didn't want you to have all the advantage while we're birding."

"Wait. Birding? You used the right word. And these…" Cassie grabbed the binoculars from his hands. "These are amazing! These are some of the best birding binoculars out there!" She held them to her eyes and scanned the ice on the river until she came to the open areas in the middle. "Look! There are some ducks out there."

"Give 'em back, and I *will* look."

"Just a sec."

Cassie suddenly felt warmth as Daniel reached across her to grab her binoculars off the bench. Her heart skipped a beat at his closeness.

"Sorry, here." She handed him his binoculars.

"No, it's fine. Go ahead. I'll use yours. What kind of ducks are we looking at?"

Cassie eagerly put the binoculars back to her eyes. "There are three different kinds I can see right off the bat."

"Where?"

"Do you see the big chunk of ice standing taller than

the rest? Right where the water starts?"

"Yes."

"Start there, and then move a little to the left. There are two ducks there."

"Hey! I see them. One has a white mohawk with a black edge on it."

Cassie smiled. "Exactly. Those are hooded mergansers."

"But they look different. Only one has the hood."

"The other is the female."

"Oh. That makes sense."

"Keep moving left. There's a group of about a dozen ducks taking turns diving under the water. See if you can identify them using the bird book."

Daniel found the ducks, and with Cassie's guidance, was able to identify common mergansers, and after them, another pair of hooded mergansers. Beyond those ducks, several mallards bobbed in the icy waves.

"This is so cool." Daniel pulled out his phone, tugged his leather glove off with his teeth, and typed the names of the ducks he'd seen into a list.

Cassie smiled. "Do you really think so? Or are you doing this for my benefit?"

"No. Really. It's cool. You're opening up a whole new world to me. I can see why you say you worship God through birdwatching."

Severe chills ran through Cassie's body—and not from the latest breeze. Could someone really understand how birding drew her closer to God? How spending time studying His creation was a form of worship? Sure, Anna was a great friend, and Cassie loved birding with her, but she wasn't a Christian. She couldn't understand this element of it. And until a few months ago, Daniel wasn't either. Could he possibly share this love with her?

"Cassie?" Daniel waved his hand in front of her face.

"Yeah?"

"I asked you what the name of your bird list is again. I can't remember what you called it."

"Oh. It's called a life list."

Daniel punched a few more keys on his phone and quickly put his glove back on. Then he pulled his own collapsible tripod out of his backpack and set it up.

"Don't tell me you bought a scope, too."

"Nope. One step at a time." He pulled a cushioned bag out of his backpack and unpacked a large DSLR camera.

"Of course. Your camera!"

Daniel grinned. "Don't leave home without it."

Cassie smiled as she indulged herself watching Daniel work *his* passion. He fastened the camera to the tripod, unpacked a long lens, attached it to the camera, and covered the whole thing with an insulating cover. When he'd lived in Toronto, he was somewhat famous. He'd photographed black-and-white landscapes and celebrities. He'd even flown around the world to do so. She hadn't known him then, though she'd seen pictures in magazines of the famed D.J. Sawyer. It didn't seem to fit with the humble, kind man sitting beside her. She'd only ever known him as small-town bookstore-owner Daniel. And that was fine with her.

"Check this out." He stepped back from the camera to allow her to look through the viewfinder.

"Wow! They're almost as close as through my scope! That's amazing!"

"Let's see if I can get some good shots."

A shadow in the sky suddenly caught Cassie's eye. She tugged on Daniel's sleeve. "Look! It's an eagle!"

They marvelled at the majestic eagle soaring above the river. It was a full adult, with the stark white head contrasting against the brown body.

"Do you see its mate?" Daniel scanned the sky.

"No. But look."

The eagle swirled downward until it came to a stop on the ice at the water's edge, upstream from the ducks.

Daniel quickly turned his camera, and Cassie her scope, until they both saw a much closer image of the beautiful raptor.

Cassie sighed. "What I wouldn't give to see that death spiral."

"Give it time. You'll get your chance."

"I certainly hope so."

"What is it about the spiral that makes you want to see it so badly?"

Cassie adjusted the focus on the scope as she continued to watch. "I don't know. The awe. The wonder. The romance."

"Romance?"

"Yeah." She leaned back and looked into Daniel's eyes. "They're partners for life. Some even say if one dies, the other will refuse to take another mate for the rest of its life. That's devotion. Love even."

"You think birds can feel love?"

"Not in the way humans can, but it's more a reflection of God's love for us."

Daniel smiled. "I understand."

And Cassie knew he meant it. Something she was still getting used to as Daniel lived out his newfound faith.

Her heart skipped another beat.

Chapter 4

After all the fresh air yesterday, Cassie had slept well. Her pre-church breakfast with Grams had filled her tummy, and the worship and message at church filled her soul.

Now, she joined Daniel on another trek to Zach and Anna's. This time with a different visitor in tow.

"Rowr!" Pumpkin howled from inside the cat carrier.

Cassie reached back from the passenger seat and straightened the blanket over the top of the carrier. "I know, baby. Don't worry. It's a short drive!"

Daniel steered his SUV around a corner. "I thought you told Anna Pumpkin travels well."

"She does. In buildings. She's never liked riding in

a vehicle."

"Do you really think she'll be able to coax Anna's cat out of hiding?"

"I'm not sure. But it's worth a shot. I don't want Anna to deal with any more stress than necessary. It can't be good for the baby."

"Hopefully, after today, the baby will have a place to sleep."

"Rowr!" Pumpkin howled again.

"Almost there!" Cassie put her hand under the blanket to stick her finger into the cage and pet Pumpkin's neck. "It's nice of you to help Zach out with the crib again today."

"I don't mind. Like Pastor David said this morning, God wants us to show His love to others. Besides, I like Zach." Daniel pulled into the driveway of Zach and Anna's house. "Except he's not here."

"Maybe he ran out for a sec. I'll text Anna." Cassie pulled out her phone and thumbed a quick message to her friend. A second later, a reply popped on the screen. "Uh oh. Looks like they had baby brain. They forgot we were coming at two. They're on their way back from the grocery store in Kemptville, and they'll be here in twenty minutes."

Daniel turned around to look at the derelict mansion across the street. "That gives us just enough time to board up the window again. And maybe do some more exploring first."

"Are you serious?" Cassie shoved her phone into

her coat's inside pocket. "You can't really mean to go back in there after that old man yelled at us."

"I did promise him I would take care of the board. Maybe it needs some fastening from inside the house."

"Rowr!"

Cassie laughed. "Even Pumpkin doesn't believe that. Go ahead if you want. I'm not leaving her alone in the cold. Leave the SUV running, please."

"Nice try. I know you want to go back in just as much as I do."

Cassie bit her lip and looked out the window at the neighbour's houses on either side of Zach and Anna's. Both seemed quiet, but there was no way to tell if someone was actually home. "What if that old man calls the cops?"

"Then we'll say 'hello' to our friend Brent." Daniel opened the vehicle door.

"I can't leave Pumpkin alone!"

"So bring her with you. It'll only be for a few minutes."

Cassie squeezed her eyes shut and shook her head. "I can't believe I'm doing this." She hopped out of the SUV and opened the back door to grab the carrier. She grunted as she lifted it.

"How about I take her?" Daniel smirked and grabbed the carrier from Cassie.

"Thanks."

Continually looking over her shoulder, Cassie followed Daniel through the snow imprints from yesterday to the front porch. They quickly skirted around the side and over to the window, hoping to get inside before Pumpkin's howls announced their criminal behaviour to the whole neighbourhood.

Daniel handed Cassie the cat carrier, climbed through the window, and then took Pumpkin back. After he set the carrier on the floor, he helped Cassie climb through.

"Whew." Cassie brushed her curls away from her face. "Is it colder in here than yesterday?"

"Well, the window has been open all night."

"Very funny." Cassie looked around at all the other openings, holes and cracks. She directed her attention to Pumpkin, lifting the blanket for a quick peek. "How are you? We won't be long, Pumpky." She picked up the carrier to take with her. "Where first?"

"How about the dining room or the kitchen?"

"Lead the way."

Daniel passed through a doorway into a grand dining room. The table and chairs were still in place, but only spiders had used them lately, by the looks of the cobwebs. A china cabinet still had dishes in it, but the glass was broken, and some of the plates were chipped. More spray-painted words and art decorated the wall.

"Nothing too interesting here. Let's keep going." Daniel continued through the next doorway into the kitchen.

Cupboards lined the wall, some open, and some with doors hanging by one hinge. Old food boxes and containers lay strewn about, covering the counter and floors.

"I guess the squirrels and raccoons were well fed over the years." Daniel kicked an old pasta container.

"Look at these!" Cassie set Pumpkin on the floor and picked up an old cocoa tin. "I can still make out the lettering and the picture. This is cool!"

Daniel opened a few cupboards. "There are still dishes in here. Look at this old Tupperware! My mother has this bowl."

"It's like a time capsule, not a museum." Cassie set the box on the counter and picked the carrier back up. "Let's see what's upstairs."

"Are you sure? We probably shouldn't be in here, you know."

Cassie glared at Daniel as he laughed.

They left the kitchen and headed back through the dining room to get to the grand staircase in the front room.

The first step creaked as Daniel stepped on it. "Careful going up. I'm not sure how safe these stairs are."

"I'm sure it's fine. The stairs in my building are older than these."

"Yes, but your building has been taken care of. Do you want me to carry Pumpkin?"

Cassie held the carrier with both hands. "Yeah, maybe. I guess I'm a little out of shape."

"Or…"

"Don't say it! She's *fluffy*."

Daniel grinned and took the carrier. Cassie felt her cheeks warm as she pictured what his flexing biceps must look like beneath his winter coat. He carefully ascended the stairs with Cassie at his heels.

As they emerged on the second floor, they were greeted by hallway décor of peeled wallpaper and more spray-painted graffiti designs. Four large rooms stood off the hall, doors open, revealing four-post beds and old quilts.

She dashed into a bedroom and gasped. "Look at this!" An old bookcase, filled with warped and weathered books, stood against the far wall. "It's such a shame."

"I'll say." Daniel switched the cat carrier to his other hand and grabbed a book. "Look. It's an old copy of *Robinson Crusoe*."

"And *Gone with the Wind*."

"Rowr!"

Cassie lifted the blanket to check on Pumpkin again. "Sorry. We'll go soon." The cat held its ears flat and glared at her.

"Let's keep moving." Daniel turned to leave the room, but his foot caught on an upturned board. He tripped, fell to his knees, and sent the cat carrier flying.

"Daniel! Pumpkin!" Cassie didn't know who to go to first. Daniel groaned but started to get to his feet. Pumpkin, however, was a different story. She howled and scratched at the bent door of the carrier. "Are you okay, kitty? I'm coming!"

Cassie ran to the cat, but as she reached the carrier, the cat busted through the door and took off out of the room. "Pumpkin! No!" She turned to Daniel.

"I'm fine. Go get her!"

Cassie ran out to the hall, but the cat was nowhere to be seen. "Pumpkin? Here kitty!" She peeked into the next bedroom. "Where'd you go? C'mon Pumpkin!"

Daniel walked in, wiping the dust from the knees of his jeans. "Can't find her?"

"Not yet. The fall must have really scared her. Normally she comes when I call."

"Sorry."

"It's all right. It was an accident. How about you? Are your knees okay?"

"I'm not as limber as I used to be, but I think I'll survive. Let's find your cat."

Cassie searched the third bedroom while Daniel looked in the fourth.

"Not in here," he called.

They met in the hallway. Cassie frowned. "Let's look again. I don't think she would've run downstairs." She peered over the railing.

"All right. You recheck those two rooms. Maybe she's hiding behind something."

"She's not under the beds. They're so high you can see right underneath them."

"For once, she can actually fit under a bed." Daniel snickered.

"Not funny." Cassie returned to the second bedroom. It only held a bed, a dresser and a closet. Even though it had been shut, she pulled the closet door open just in case.

Nothing.

Daniel met her in the third bedroom, but the results were the same. One dresser, one bed, and a closet. This room also had a chair, but clearly, no cat was underneath or behind it.

"Let me just check this closet too. The door is open an inch."

"She needs more than an inch to—"

"Stop now," Cassie muttered as she pulled the door open.

Except it wasn't a closet, entirely. Beyond a bar with wire hangers and a couple of old coats, a skinny set of stairs led to an attic.

"Oh." Daniel scratched the back of his neck. "That's interesting."

"Pumpkin! Are you up there! Here kitty, kitty!"

"Do you want me to go first?"

Cassie nodded, fighting back the tears. Now she was starting to worry.

Metal on metal screeched as Daniel slid an old coat on a wire hanger out of the way, and started up the stairs. They were creaky, and the boards were warped but seemed to hold his weight no problem. She followed him, a few steps behind.

At the top, the staircase ended under a little dormer.

Daniel had to duck to take the last step. He turned to give Cassie a hand to step onto the rickety floor.

Only a bit of light came through the dormers and the few holes in the ceiling. She turned and took a few steps to where there was headroom and turned on her phone's flashlight. The attic was filled with old trunks, crates, dressers and piles of boxes, providing plenty of places for a cat to hide—even a large one. Some stacks were water damaged from the holes above, but everything was also coated in a large dust layer.

"Look!" Cassie pointed her flashlight to the floor, where fresh kitty pawprints tracked through the dirt. "She's here! Pumpkin!"

Carefully following the prints and keeping an eye on the floorboards for footing, Cassie wound between the boxes and trunks until she emerged in a second part of the attic. She quickly scanned the room with her light until an odd shape came into focus in front of her.

She screamed.

"What? What is it?" Daniel was at her side in seconds.

Cassie continued to point the light ahead of her. A skeleton hung from a noose, a few torn shards of a sixties dress with a psychedelic pattern lay on the floor beneath it.

"Call Brent. Immediately."

Chapter 5

Officer Brent Adams appeared at the window opening and aimed his heavy-duty flashlight back and forth between Cassie and Daniel's eyes, then scanned the ceiling of the room.

"Hey, guys. Where's the body?"

Cassie crossed her arms and bit her lip. "It's a skeleton, actually. Not much body left."

"A skeleton? Really?" Lexy appeared beside Brent. His eyes lit up when he saw her.

"Hey. Sorry to call you out on a Sunday. Just thought you'd want to be here since it was Cassie and Daniel who made the call."

"Of course. Thank you." Lexy smiled and batted her eyelashes.

Brent aimed his flashlight at the front door. "Wanna unlock that so we don't have to climb through the window?"

Cassie shook her head. "Tried. The lock is either rusted or frozen. It won't budge."

"Okay, then." Brent climbed through the window and helped Lexy in after him.

"Thanks for coming." Daniel rubbed the back of his neck.

"I am the police. I kinda have to."

"You know what I mean. The body's in the attic."

"The attic?" Brent aimed the light up the stairs. "What were you guys doing up there? Or in here at all, for that matter?" He scanned the room again.

Daniel looked away and whistled.

Cassie nudged him with her elbow. "We were exploring, and Pumpkin got away. We found the attic while we were searching for her."

"Pumpkin? Why would you have her here?" Brent furrowed his brows and shook his head as if trying to jumble the story together in his brain.

"Here's the short version." Cassie dropped her shoulders. "Zach and Anna moved across the street. Daniel and I and—"

Lexy shook her head and stared wide-eyed at Cassie from behind Brent.

"Daniel and I," Cassie continued. "Came here yesterday to take a peek inside. I've always loved this mansion. The board was loose on the window, so we came in but left after one of the crotchety old neighbours yelled at us." She shifted her weight from one foot to the other. "Then we returned today to repair the board properly but couldn't resist another peek. I had Pumpkin with me in a carrier because we were waiting for Zach and Anna to get back so our cats could visit. I didn't want to leave her in the car, so we brought her in."

"I was carrying her, and I tripped," Daniel said. "The cage broke, and she got loose. She ran to the attic, and that's where we saw the skeleton."

"Where is she now?"

Cassie pointed to the wall facing the street. "At Zach and Anna's. We caught her after we called you and thought it best to bring her there while we waited for you to come."

"All right then." Brent pointed the light. "Lead the way. Should be fun trying to identify a person from skeletal remains."

"Oh, we know who it is." Cassie ran to the little side table to grab the picture frame Daniel had cleaned off the day before. "It's this lady."

Brent grabbed the picture. "How do you know?"

"She went missing years ago. Or ran away, as the rumour goes. Lexy knows the story better than I do."

Lexy nodded.

"And there are a few worn remnants of the same dress on the floor underneath the skeleton."

The crotchety old neighbour appeared in the

window frame, the ear flaps on his hat blowing in the breeze. "I hope you're here to arrest these troublemakers!"

"Hi, Edward." Brent approached the old man.

"You know him?" Cassie whispered.

"Guys, this is Edward Morris. He *often* helps the village by reporting nuisances."

"These three *are* nuisances. Trespassing two days in a row! I warned them I would call you. Looks like someone beat me to it."

"*Three?*" Brent turned to Lexy. She smiled and shrugged.

"I hope you lock 'em up, Brent."

"Don't worry, Ed. I have it under control. You can go home now."

Edward waved his hand and stormed off, muttering to himself.

"Let's get this taken care of." Brent flicked his flashlight aiming the beam up the stairs again, then paused to look at Lexy. "And you and I will talk later."

She gave him a sheepish grin.

Daniel led the way up the staircase, through the little bedroom closet, and up the skinny attic stairs. Then they carefully maneuvered around the trunks and crates, paying close attention to each step on the shaky attic floorboards.

"Ew!" Lexy wrinkled her nose.

"Yup. She's dead." Brent chuckled.

Lexy elbowed him. "Not funny. This is a real person

we're talking about."

"Right. Sorry. You three sit there while I take a look." He pointed to a row of crates.

"So, how does this fit into the story you told us, Lex?" Cassie wiped the crate with her mitten before she sat.

"I think it makes perfect sense. He left after the argument, and she was so distraught she decided she couldn't live without him."

"You think it's that simple?" Daniel asked.

"Nothing about suicide is ever simple."

Cassie tilted her head and observed Brent as he examined different parts of the skeleton. "She must have really loved him to do something so desperate."

"Of course, you'd try and make this romantic." Daniel rolled his eyes.

"It's not romantic. At all. But it's true. Imagine a love so deep, one person can't dream about living without the other."

"That's a deep love," Daniel said.

"But misdirected in the end. That's not how God wants things to turn out. Marriage is a picture of the love He wants us to have for Him. We, His people, the church, are His bride." Cassie turned and met Daniel's eyes. Once again, they penetrated her soul. Her heart sped up, so she looked away. Now wasn't the time to muddle through the puzzle of her feelings for him.

"Do you need any equipment from the car or the office?" Lexy approached Brent.

"Not yet. But maybe you can shine the light here for me." Brent poked at a piece of worn cloth stuck to the skeleton's hip.

"Yuck." Cassie turned away.

"Definitely not romantic." Daniel grimaced.

"No," Cassie agreed. "It's really sad."

"It's horrible." Lexy moved the light to follow Brent's hands as he took a closer look at the ribs. "The poor woman. All alone—and then trapped up here for years with no proper burial or people to grieve her."

Daniel grimaced. "Didn't she have parents? Or friends? No one questioned her whereabouts?"

Lexy shook her head. "Not as the story goes. Everyone thought she'd left to start a new life somewhere. No one could find her, so they assumed she was the one who cut them off."

Brent rummaged through the stack of fallen crates beneath the skeleton. He picked a strong-looking square one and hopped onto it. "Pass me the light, please." He held out his hand.

Lexy obliged and stepped back toward Cassie and Daniel. "It makes sense if you think about it. They couldn't find her, and no one ever received word from her. It would be easier to be angry at her and assume she'd written them off than it would be to assume she was dead."

"But these are all still rumours, right?" Cassie asked. "If this happened in the sixties, it's safe to say the story's been twisted and changed since then."

"Maybe, but I think there are still a few people around from back then who remember what happened."

Cassie frowned. "I meant to do some research last night after birding, but I was too tired when I got home. I ended up cuddling on the couch with Pumpkin and a cozy mystery someone gave me." She smiled at Daniel. He kept her in good supply of books.

"I'll see what I can dig up for you."

"Thanks, Lex." Cassie had relied on Lexy for information a few times in the past. Not because she worked at the police station, but because she was skilled at finding out information on the internet through social profiles and news articles. Although her access to police files didn't hurt, Cassie didn't like asking her friend to put her job on the line for information. They resorted to legal ways as much as possible.

Brent hopped off the crate and picked up another, smaller one. When he shook it, a board came loose, so he grabbed another one instead. He set it on top of the first big crate and climbed up them like stairs.

"Be careful!" Lexy called to him.

Brent didn't answer her. His focus was on the skeleton in front of him, and the stone-cold look on his face made it clear no one could interrupt him. He reached up to touch the rafter the rope hung around, then aimed the light at the skull in front of him. The air was thick with dust sparkling in the light beam.

"Just as I thought." He looked at the others.

"What's wrong?" Lexy asked. "Do you need the kit now? Or something else?"

"We need more than a kit. We need a forensics unit."

"What? Why?"

"Come see."

Cassie followed Lexy and Daniel around to the other side of the skeleton where Brent stood.

"Can you see it from down there?" Brent pointed his flashlight at the back of the skull."

"It looks like a little hole." Cassie squinted.

"It is."

"So?" Daniel asked.

"This little hole is from blunt force trauma to the head."

Lexy stood on her tiptoes to try and get a better look even though the skull was several feet up. "Did she have an accident or a concussion sometime in her life?"

Cassie shook her head. "Nope. If that happened during her lifetime, the edges would be smooth and show signs of healing. Am I right?"

Brent nodded. "These edges are sharp and were fresh at the time of death."

Daniel glanced back and forth between Brent and Cassie. "What are you saying?"

Cassie put her hand on her hip. "It appears Miss Sixties-Dress didn't hang herself. She was murdered."

"And hung here after to make it appear like a suicide." Brent lowered the light.

"But how could someone do that?" Lexy asked. "Wouldn't there be blood on her head? How could the murderer have hidden it?"

Cassie shrugged. "Stopped the bleeding and washed her hair?"

"Something like that." Brent hopped down. "But one thing's for certain."

"What?" Daniel asked.

"We're standing in the middle of a crime scene."

Chapter 6

A sudden noise jarred Cassie out of her dream of skeletons dancing to sixties music and back into the realm of consciousness. She tried to move but realized she was pinned down. Where was she? Her mind struggled to get its bearings while her eyes gathered up the energy to open. Ah, right. She was home. Her late Sunday afternoon reading break-turned-nap. But why couldn't she move? She forced her eyes open.

"Pumpkin!"

The cat sat on Cassie's hip and thigh. Not only did she have Cassie pinned down, but she'd also cut off the circulation and Cassie's whole leg was numb.

"Silly kitty! You have to move. Sorry." She nudged the cat, who continued to ignore her.

Cassie's phone buzzed, and the vibration made it dance on the table. It was Daniel.

I'm in the bookstore finishing up a few things. Gonna order pizza. Want to join me?

Cassie couldn't help but smile. *Sure. Be down in a few. K.*

"Now you really have to get up, kitty." Cassie struggled underneath the cat's weight to sit up and slide Pumpkin onto the blanket.

"Rowr!"

"Sorry. Gotta go see Daniel. Wanna come?"

Pumpkin's ears twitched. Cassie laughed. She knew when she was ready to leave, Pumpkin would be waiting at the door. She always accompanied Cassie to her store downstairs and often went to the bookstore with her for impromptu visits with Daniel.

She was also glad Pumpkin had successfully coaxed Anna's cat, Caramel, out of hiding. By the time Cassie had picked Pumpkin up to go home, Caramel was sitting on the sofa playing with his toy mouse.

Cassie sighed and wondered how the investigation was going. The forensics team had just arrived as Daniel and Cassie were leaving. It would be a while before she'd hear anything, but she knew Lexy would text as soon as there was news.

Cassie tried to tame her curly hair in front of the mirror, but it refused to cooperate. Finally, she managed to pull part of it back and let a few loose curls hang around her face. She put a long, navy hoodie over her tight leggings, and to finish the outfit, shoved woollen slipper boots onto her feet. Her makeup needed little refreshing, but she put on some pale lipstick. It was an effort to appear Sunday casual but still make sure she looked her best for Daniel.

Cassie balked at the thought. Why would that matter? She wouldn't do this to go see Lexy or Anna. So, why the concern over her looks to go see Daniel? Somehow, the line of friendship had been crossed again, and she needed to pull in the reins. She pulled the elastic out of her hair and put it all into a simple ponytail instead.

"Ready, Pumpkin?"

The cat met Cassie at the door and bounded ahead of her down the stairs. By the time Cassie arrived at the bookshop's door in the hallway, Pumpkin was already there, scratching at the doorframe.

Cassie knocked once and let herself in. The Book Nook was one of her favourite places to be. The long store had old, wooden bookcases lining the walls, with more cases protruding outward to make little nooks. An antique bar-turned-cash counter stood in the front corner, and at the back of the store, a cozy fireplace surrounded by comfy chairs offered a quiet spot to read. Deep-silled windows lined the far stone wall between the book nooks, currently decorated with greenery, wooden snowflakes, and hurricane lamps. As usual, Daniel had the white mini lights on, and the rest of the lights dimmed. Soft worship music played in the background.

Daniel was crouched over a box of books when he saw her. "You made it!" He dropped books into the box and jumped to his feet. He beamed from ear to ear.

"Of course. I'm hungry after our little adventure today."

"So, you're just here for the food?"

"And maybe a tea."

"Oh. Well, to get the tea, you'll have to participate in at least ten minutes of casual conversation."

Cassie giggled. "What if I want two teas?"

"That'll cost you."

"Rowr!" Pumpkin rubbed against Daniel's feet.

"Hey, kitty." He bent down to scratch her ear.

Cassie stepped up to Daniel. "Now the tables have turned. You now owe *me* for the privilege of petting Pumpkin."

"Well worth it." Daniel stood and leaned forward, so close Cassie could feel his breath on her face. "How may I be of service, m'lady?"

Tingles ran up and down Cassie's arms. She gulped. He was so close she could easily lean in and kiss him. Why did that thought enter her mind? She quickly stepped back. "I'll think about it and let you know."

Daniel's smile lessened as he backed away, but his gaze held hers. "Whenever you're ready."

She gulped again. He was clearly addressing their relationship. "Daniel—"

"Let me finish with these books, and I'll order the

pizza. Where do you want me to get it from?"

"Wood Oven Pizza, of course." Cassie grinned, relieved he'd changed the subject. "Why are you working today, anyway? You do remember our stores are closed on Sundays in the winter?"

"I know. I just wanted to finish up a few things. And I like the quiet."

"I understand. It's peaceful in here."

"Thanks. Have you heard from Lexy yet? Any news from the crime scene?" Daniel pulled three copies of an autobiography out of the box.

"No. I imagine they won't be done for a while."

"I can't believe you've stumbled upon another murder."

Cassie sighed. "Me either."

"There goes your romantic notion of the mansion, too."

"I'm guessing it was the husband who did it. So, still a crime of passion. But yeah, not the way love should go. I still love the house, though."

"You think it's the husband?"

"Surely. Who else would it be? They had a fight. He killed her and left."

Daniel placed a few books on a table with a sale sign. "Do you think he's still alive?"

"Wow. I never thought of that. I suppose he could be."

"Brent will find out, I guess."

"We don't even know the lady's name." Cassie

plopped into a nearby armchair and hung her leg over the side. "I need to think of her as something other than *Miss Sixties-Dress*."

"Let's see what we can find." Daniel knelt on the floor beside the chair and leaned over the arm with his phone.

Cassie turned and placed both her feet flat on the floor. Daniel's familiar scent of leather and old books penetrated her nose. She ignored her speeding heartbeat. "What are you going to search?"

"Uh…" He scratched his head and typed as he spoke, "Elm Street, Banford."

Results filled the screen. Daniel scrolled past real estate listings, garage sale ads, garbage route information and a daycare ad, but nothing seemed to pertain to the old mansion.

"What if you typed in the house number?"

"Maybe." Daniel popped over to his map app, looked up the number, and added it to the search. Nothing different came up. "Any other ideas?"

"Banford weddings in the sixties?"

"How will that help if we don't know who we're looking for?"

"Ugh." Cassie slumped her shoulders. "This is why Lexy does most of the internet research for me. I don't even know where to start with this one."

Daniel lowered his phone and placed a hand on her shoulder. He massaged it a little. "We'll just have to wait until she calls. Let me make you a tea." He walked over to the coffee bar set up in one of the window nooks.

Cassie placed a hand on her coat where his had been, and traces of the electricity ran down her spine. Why did his touch always do that to her? "Thank you." She heard him pop a pod into the machine and listened while the water ran into the mug.

A moment later, he appeared beside her with her tea. "Let's sit by the fire where it's cozier." He nudged his head to the roaring fire.

"Sure," Cassie agreed, not positive she should be thinking about getting even *more* cozy with Daniel today. But she followed him anyway. As she sat and took the hot mug of tea, her phone buzzed. "It's Lexy!"

"Are they done?"

Cassie quickly scanned the text. "No. Won't be for a while. But she did some research for Brent while he was working the scene." Another text came through. "They do think it's the lady in the photo you found but can't say for certain until after the autopsy and dental record search are completed. Her name was Marilyn Howard. Her husband, Wayne, is still alive and still owns the house. He lives in Ottawa and is coming to the station tomorrow for an interview. Though he doesn't yet know why."

"Wow." Daniel raised his eyebrows. "He *is* still alive. That's crazy!"

"It is."

"To think you've gotten away with murder, only to have it resurface this many years later. How do they know he won't bolt?"

Cassie shrugged. "They don't seem to be worried. And anyway, they're only assuming he did it."

"You did, too. You said so earlier."

"It makes the most sense. But if it wasn't him, I'm going to help find out who it was."

Daniel turned and looked into her eyes. "Why the sudden urgency? What's changed?"

"Now she has a name. She's a real person. And her life was ended unfairly. That house was meant for romance and dreams—not death."

He tucked a curl behind her ear. "And I know you'll help Brent figure it out."

Cassie struggled to look away from Daniel's gaze. Something about the words *romance* and *dreams* really resonated in her soul while she looked at him. How had she crossed the line so quickly again? She jumped up and pulled her phone from her pocket. "Let's order the pizza. I'm starved."

Chapter 7

Cassie scurried around Olde Crow Primitives, dusting the displays of candles, rustic wooden signs, lanterns, and other country décor. She wanted to finish the cleaning before Grams came in for her shift at eleven. Then she'd be free to pop over to the police office by eleven-fifteen when Wayne Howard was due for his interview.

Lexy had tried to talk her out of it, but Cassie had insisted. Hearing things firsthand was always better than hearing a shortened rendition. Besides, Cassie wanted to see what Mr. Howard looked like.

The station was only a satellite office, which, until Brent came on as Banford's full-time officer a couple of months ago, was only used once a week. It was very tiny with only the front counter, a couple of chairs, and a single office.

If everything went according to plan, Cassie would arrive at the station just after Mr. Howard entered Brent's office. Lexy would leave the door open and make sure to sit in the far chair, leaving the chair by the door for Mr. Howard. Brent would be unable to see Cassie from his spot behind the desk.

But she would hear everything.

She felt a twinge of guilt at her plan but quickly justified her actions by remembering how Brent had included her in his last murder investigation. She'd even done some undercover work for him—of sorts. Surely, he wouldn't get angry at her for happening to be in the office while he interviewed this murder suspect. Would he?

The bells hanging above the store door rang as two older ladies entered.

"Hello!" Cassie waved. "Nice to see you this morning."

"You too, dear." The one with a purplish hair colour answered.

The larger, more robust of the two approached the cash counter. "Is that cat of yours here today?"

"She sure is." Cassie put down her duster and went behind the cash area to grab Pumpkin from her sleeping box and set her on top of the counter.

"Rowr?" Pumpkin looked at the lady and immediately rubbed against her outstretched hand.

"Come see the kitty, Ethel."

The purple-haired lady approached the counter, and her eyes opened wide. "Woah. She's one big kitty."

"More to love, that's what I always say," the robust woman said.

"You would say that, Jean."

Cassie chuckled and returned to her dusting, leaving the two ladies to pet Pumpkin and browse the store.

Moments later, the bell rang again as Grams arrived. "Jean! How are you, my friend?" She gave the large woman a hug.

Of course, Grams knew her. Grams knew everyone in Banford. Which is one of the reasons she wanted to stay on working at the store after she'd sold the building to Cassie. She loved people and wanted to continue seeing and visiting with them.

Speaking of which, Cassie had people of her own to *see*. And listen to. Even though Grams hadn't taken her coat off yet, Cassie grabbed her own down-filled jacket and put it on.

As she walked by Grams, Jean and Ethel, she waved. "Hi, Grams. I have an errand to run. I'll be about an hour. Do you mind?"

"Of course, dear. You go right ahead." She gave her best smile, which lit up her grey eyes and, along with her spiky grey hairstyle, made her look twenty years younger.

Cassie skipped out and made her way down the street to the Banford Municipal Offices. The police satellite office was attached to the side of the building complex.

She checked her phone to see it was already ten minutes past eleven. Cassie assumed Wayne Howard should be arriving about now. Did people actually arrive late to interviews at the police station? She didn't think so. Picking up the pace, she scurried down the street.

As she rounded the bend and the police office came into view, a tall man in a business suit and a long, black overcoat closed the door of his fancy Lexus. He had white hair, combed neatly to the side, and a neatly trimmed beard covered his pointed chin. Cassie guessed him to be in his seventies. It must be Wayne Howard.

Sure enough, he entered the police building. Cassie slowed her pace, allowing time for Brent to invite the man into his office. A few minutes later, she quietly opened the door and carefully pulled it shut behind her.

She grinned. Her timing had been perfect. The three sat in Brent's office, with the door left ajar. When she took a seat in the farthest chair, she had an excellent view of the back of Wayne's head and part of his face. He wouldn't see her unless he turned around.

And she could hear them perfectly.

"Of course," Wayne said. "No problem at all. Could you tell me what this is about?"

Cassie heard Brent clear his throat. "You own the mansion on Elm Street?"

Wayne nodded. "Oh. I see. I bet it's a real eyesore by now. Am I violating by-laws?"

"No, no. Nothing like that. When's the last time you were there?"

"It's been… years."

"How many years?"

"I haven't been there since I left in sixty-eight."

"May I ask why you left?"

Wayne gulped. "I, uh…" He forced out a sigh. "I left my wife. I walked out and never looked back."

"And what did she do after that?"

"I'm really not sure. I heard rumours she left, too. But I decided to leave the house as it was, so it was there for her if she ever changed her mind and wanted to go back."

Cassie heard tapping. Brent must have been bouncing his pen on the desk.

"You never spoke to her again?"

"No, I…" Wayne ran his hand through his hair, messing it up. "Why are you asking me these questions? What's going on?"

"I think you need to be a little more forthcoming with your answers. There's more to your story, and we need you to tell it."

"Why? What happened?"

"Is this your wife?"

Wayne grabbed a picture from Brent's outstretched hand. He lowered his head and stared at the photo a moment before responding. "Yes. That's Marilyn."

"We found Marilyn hanging from a noose in the attic. The coroner confirmed this morning it was her."

"What?" The picture slid from Wayne's hand and fell to his lap. "When? How long?"

"It appears she was wearing the same dress as in that photo, so probably since 1968."

Wayne picked it up again and stared at it. "Marilyn... my dear Marilyn..." He sniffed.

Cassie put her hand on her heart. The poor man. Maybe he hadn't done it.

"Why did you leave, Wayne? What was the fight about?" Brent continued.

Wayne rubbed his forehead and then ran his hand over his face to wipe away a tear. "All right, all right." He continued to stare at the photo as he spoke. "She'd had an affair." He sobbed. "I found out, and we had a huge fight. I was devastated. We were newly married—only three years. She was the world to me, but I was often gone for work. I wasn't there when she needed me."

Cassie shook her head. An affair? That added a whole other level to the story. The rumours hadn't mentioned an affair.

"Then what happened?" Brent continued.

"I packed a suitcase and left. I didn't mean to stay away for long. I'd only intended to think for a few days. But the more I thought about it, the more furious I became. One day turned into two, then three, and before I knew it, a couple of weeks had flown by."

"So, you were very angry with Marilyn."

"No, not at her. At the man she'd had an affair with.

He must have known she was married. How could he do that to another man's wife?"

"You weren't mad at Marilyn herself?"

Wayne shook his head. "Not for long, anyway. Like I said, I wasn't there for her when she needed me. She wasn't to blame. Not really. She was young and impressionable. The man took advantage of her."

Cassie wrinkled her brows. If he loved her so much, why hadn't he made time for her?

Brent pressed on. "Who was the man she had an affair with?"

"I… I don't know. I never found out."

"And why didn't you ever go back?"

He shrugged. "I blamed myself for the affair. I was embarrassed and ashamed that my wife had to turn elsewhere for comfort."

"And when did you realize she wasn't at the house, either? Don't tell me it was through a rumour. Tell me the truth."

"A couple months later. A friend of mine called to tell me. I figured she'd go back, eventually. I wanted her to… to have the house. So, I kept making the tax payments."

Brent's chair scraped across the floor. "You're telling me that you've been paying the taxes on the place since 1968, and you've never returned?"

Keyboard keys clicked.

"Yup," Lexy piped up. "Taxes have been paid in full every year."

Cassie smiled. Lexy had worked in the municipal office before she started working full-time for Brent. She must still have access to those records.

"Look." Wayne placed his hand on the desk. "I know it sounds strange. But Marilyn was the love of my life. The whole affair was not only embarrassing but devastating. I never dated another woman after that. I've been alone since then, and I've worked crazy hours to compensate by building a business. The money for the taxes was trivial. In fact, I haven't even thought about it for years and years. My accountant takes care of it for me. Though I've thought of Marilyn most every day."

Brent and Lexy remained silent. Cassie knew this was probably Brent's way of getting the suspect to confess more.

"I never should've left." Wayne buried his head in his hands. "Or at least, I should've returned the next day. I regret it. I've regretted it every day of my life. But as the years passed, it became harder and harder to ever go back, and I didn't know where to look even if I'd wanted to find her. By the time I figured out she was probably never going back to the house either, I didn't want to deal with it anymore. I knew I wouldn't be able to bear seeing the place."

He grabbed the photo from the desk and cradled it in his hand. "And all this time. She *was* there." He sobbed. "Oh, Marilyn. I'm so sorry!"

"What are you sorry about, exactly?" Brent asked.

"That I left her. I was shattered by what happened, but obviously, she was even more hurt than I. How could she have? How could…" Another sob. "All these years, and it never occurred to me she'd ended her own life."

"Oh, did I say that?"

"What do you mean?" Wayne looked up.

"I never said she ended her own life, Wayne. Marilyn was murdered."

Wayne's mouth hung agape as he slowly placed the photo back on the desk a second time. "Mur… murdered? But you said—"

"I said she was hanging from a noose—which she was. But someone murdered her before they hung her there."

"And you think… you think… I?"

"I haven't said what I think. I'm just asking questions right now."

Wayne sniffed again and wiped tears from his face.

"Let me get you some tissue." Brent's chair scraped across the floor again.

"I'll get it. I'll get it!" Lexy squeaked.

But it was too late. Brent opened the door, headed to the counter, and looked up. He froze when he saw Cassie sitting there.

She gulped and offered an apologetic smile. "Uh… hi?"

Chapter 8

"What are you doing here?" Brent whispered. "Or do I even need to ask?"

Cassie shrugged. "I came by to see how the investigation's going."

Brent placed his hands flat on the counter and took a deep breath. "How convenient of you to come by at *exactly* the time of my interview with the victim's husband."

"Oh? Is that who you're in there with?"

"As if you didn't know."

Cassie gave a sheepish grin. "Sorry."

"If you and Lexy keep pushing the boundaries like this, her job could be on the line. And so could mine."

"Please don't do anything rash. It's not Lexy's fault.

I can't help myself. I want justice for that poor woman."

"I understand that." Brent's shoulders relaxed. "I do, too. But there are ethical ways to go about it. I'd love your help on this. You're an intelligent woman. But please, don't force me to compromise my position, or Lexy's."

Cassie's cheeks warmed. She was a Christian. She was supposed to be a moral example to others, not be criticized for lack of ethics. "I'm truly sorry. It won't happen again." She stood and made her way to the door.

"Cassie," Brent called.

She turned back.

"Thanks for understanding. I'll have Lexy get in touch with you later."

Cassie nodded and let herself out. She said a silent prayer on the short trek back to Olde Crow Primitives, asking God for forgiveness. Brent was right. She'd crossed the line one too many times. First and foremost, she served God. Her job was to make Him known through her actions and her words. Justice was important too, as it also was to Him, but she had to be sure to honour the Lord while seeking it, trusting Him to help her.

By the time she arrived at work, Cassie felt refreshed and at peace.

"Got all your errands done, dear?" Grams asked as she readjusted the display of travel mugs.

Coat still on, Cassie slipped behind the counter to

give Pumpkin a quick nuzzle. "I did. Thank you."

"No problem. Had a couple of good sales while you were gone."

"On a cold, winter's Monday? Nice!"

Grams winked. "I went straight for the jugular."

"Grams!"

"Maybe I should work on commission."

Cassie laughed. "How about I buy you a doughnut and a coffee, instead?"

"Deal!"

"I'll be right back." Cassie darted back out the door and across the street to Drummond's Bakery. The smell of fresh bread and cinnamon met her on the sidewalk before she even entered the building. As she tugged the door open, the smell intensified, and her stomach roared in response. She hopped into line, and when it was her turn, ordered two Boston crème doughnuts.

Her next stop was at Java Junction to get Grams a coffee and a nice, tall, Earl Grey tea for herself. With a cup in each hand, and the bag of doughnuts dangling beneath, she exited the café just as Daniel approached and almost ran into her.

"Hey." He grinned ear-to-ear. "Fancy meeting you here."

"Hi." Her body warmed as much as the drinks in her hands.

"Are you in a rush?"

"Kind of. I was already out this morning, and I'm bringing this coffee to Grams. But I can wait in line with you, and we can walk back together."

"All the way across the street? Done. I accept."

Cassie followed Daniel back inside. "I have some news on the murder. The husband had an interview with Brent this morning."

"Is that where you were? I'm surprised he let you listen in."

"Uh… he didn't, but I overheard. And was rightfully reprimanded."

"Did he lock you up?" Daniel grinned.

"No, but I was convicted about unethical behaviour. Does that count?"

"Convicted by the Holy Spirit, you mean?"

"Yes. I'm going to tread lightly from now on."

"Good girl." Daniel put his arm around her and gave her a squeeze. "What's next on the agenda?"

"I was thinking of heading to the library after work tonight. They're open later on Mondays. Maybe they have old newspapers, school yearbooks, or town history books that mention Marilyn Howard."

"To what end?"

"I don't know. Connections? Motives? Something else that might give me an idea of who would want to murder her."

Daniel turned to the barista and ordered, "Large double-double, please." He looked back at Cassie. "It wasn't the husband?"

"I don't know. It still could be, I guess. But my gut isn't sold on the notion."

Daniel took his coffee and paid the young man. "Uh oh. That opens a whole new can of worms."

Cassie followed Daniel out of the store. "Exactly. Not what I was counting on, but I want to figure this case out."

"I could join you at the library, if you think it would help?"

They skipped in front of a slow, on-coming car. "I'd love that. Meet me at my apartment at six-thirty?"

"Sounds great. See you then." He opened the door to Olde Crow Primitives and held it open long enough for Cassie to get through. He waved to Grams before heading on his way.

Cassie's heart swelled. And she found herself humming as she worked the rest of the afternoon. Grams eyed her a few times, but opted not to say anything about Daniel. Cassie was relieved.

A few hours later, Cassie sat across from Daniel in the old, rustic log building by the Rideau River that served as the Banford library.

She loved this building. Massive logs crisscrossed the high ceiling, holding up the roof and creating space for a loft and a children's area. Windows all around gave a spectacular view of the river and the park next door. Walls and aisles of books filled the space.

"Anything?" Daniel peered across the table at the old Banford High School yearbook Cassie perused.

"Not yet. You?"

"Just the same school photo of Marilyn. I don't see

her in any other photos."

Cassie suddenly turned her book around so Daniel could see. "Is that her?" She pointed at a basketball team photo.

"Might be."

"Doesn't really help, though, does it?" She sighed and pulled the book back. "Maybe we should look through some old newspapers."

"It's worth a shot."

Cassie slid her chair backward and walked to the reception desk.

The tall, lean librarian pushed her glasses up her nose and smiled. "Need some help, Cassie?"

"Yes please, Roberta. I'd like to look through some old Banford newspapers."

"How old?" She clicked the mouse to wake her computer screen.

"Between 1965 and 1968?"

"Oh." Roberta frowned. "I'm afraid we don't have records from that long ago. Our oldest scans only go back to the eighties."

"Rats. What about hard copies? Do you have old newspapers anywhere? Ones waiting to be entered into the system?"

"Afraid not. Sorry."

"That's okay. Maybe I'll try Mrs. Dingham's Antique Shop.

Roberta shook her head. "She already donated all the old newspapers she had."

Cassie slumped her shoulders. "All right. Thanks anyway."

Daniel looked up as she returned. "Any luck?"

"No. They don't have newspapers that old." She flopped back into her chair.

"These history books don't seem to be helpful either." He snapped one shut. "Most of them talk about the bigger cities and Upper Canada. There's only a small section on Banford, and it only mentions the mill, the locks, and the doctor in the village."

"I think most of these books predate the existence of our old mansion. Even though it's one of the older buildings in town."

Daniel slid his hand across the table and gently placed it on Cassie's. "How about we get this cleaned up and take the river trail back home?"

Cassie's spirits lifted slightly at his touch. "Sure."

"Don't worry. You'll figure out another angle."

"I hope so."

They stacked the books and placed them on the return cart. Cassie thanked Roberta once again, and followed Daniel out of the library into the cold night.

Instead of following the library lane back to the street, they headed for the trail alongside the river as Daniel had suggested. The moonlight glistened off the snow and the ice, making it possible to walk without using flashlights once their eyes adjusted.

A great horned owl hooted in the distance.

"Is that your owl?" Daniel asked.

"It is!" Cassie beamed. A pair of owls were raising another brood on the Anglican Church grounds in Banford. The Bird Club, Cassie included, continually monitored their progress with a live cam Cassie had helped install last Christmas—before helping solve the previous murder in the village.

"It's certainly beautiful out here." Daniel paused to look out over the icy river.

"Very." Cassie stopped beside him to share the view. A moment later, his gloved hand wrapped around her own mittened one. She held her breath. Her arm tingled, and her heart soared.

But her head screamed at her to let go.

She gulped. What should she do? There's nothing she wanted more than to hold Daniel's hand on the walk home—even more than she wanted to see the eagles' death spiral. But she couldn't.

Not yet.

Could she?

"Cassie?" Daniel's breath formed a cloud as he spoke. "Would you go out to dinner with me on Valentine's Day?"

She let go of his hand. "Daniel—"

He raised his palms to her. "Never mind. Sorry. I shouldn't have asked." He started walking again, single file, ahead of her.

"Daniel, please."

"Please what?" He whirled around. "Please wait? Please be patient? I *have* been, Cassie."

"I know."

"Do you? Do you really know?"

Cassie swallowed the lump in her throat. "I just… can't. Not yet."

"Why? What are you waiting for?"

"I don't know! I only know I need more time."

"Okay, okay. You're right. I'm sorry. I don't want to rush you. It's just such a beautiful night. And you're so beautiful. And your heart is beautiful." Daniel touched his glove to her face. "And I'm out of line. I apologize." He shook his head.

"I'm sorry."

"Don't be. I just have to keep placing the notion of us into God's hands. He knows what's best for you and for me. I have to work on the patience thing a little more."

Was this really Daniel talking? His faith had grown so much in only a few short months. He was truly a man of God. Cassie could feel it in every fibre of her being.

So, what was her problem?

Cassie followed Daniel as he continued to walk down the trail. Whatever it was, she was sure to be up all night thinking about it—and an old murder.

Chapter 9

Cassie stomped the snow off her boots on the mat inside The Tea Garden's door and waved to Lexy and Maggie, already seated at the café table by the window. The girls had a weekly breakfast date Tuesday mornings before work. It was a high point in Cassie's week, a time she'd come to enjoy and value with her best friend and sister-in-law.

A berry muffin called out to Cassie from behind the glass display window, and she ordered an Earl Grey tea to go along with it. The tea was served in a pretty teacup with pink flowers. She carefully took hold of the saucer and carried it to her table, admiring the décor.

"Hi, Ladies." Cassie sat and smelled the pink roses

in front of her. "Isn't this cute?"

This month, the tea shop had been decorated to reflect Valentine's Day. To play on the lace and Victorian themes, hearts and roses had been added to the flower vases, window display, and table centrepieces.

"Very." Lexy finished sipping her tea. "And for once, I'm looking forward to Valentine's Day."

"Oh?" Maggie asked. "Got a hot date?"

A grin stretched across Lexy's face. "Brent asked me to dinner."

"Finally," Cassie smirked. "It's about time you two stopped flirting all the time and actually went out."

Both Maggie and Lexy froze and stared at Cassie.

"What?"

"Look who's talking." Maggie's bobbed hair danced as she shook her head.

"Hardly the same situation. Where's he taking you, Lex?"

"He made reservations at The Inn in Oxford Mills. It's so romantic there."

"I'm surprised he got in." Cassie tore another piece off her muffin. "You have to book weeks ahead to get in there for Valentine's."

Lexy's eyes lit up. "That's right. So, he must have…" She hunched her shoulders and giggled.

"Good thing you said, yes." Maggie grinned.

"Are you sure about this, though? With Brent? Have you guys talked about faith?" Cassie eyed her friend with concern. As much as she wanted Lexy to be happy, it was more important that she be with someone who shared her faith. God required it. "You know what Grams always says. Be with someone who loves God more than you, and you more than himself."

"She has a point," Maggie agreed.

"Don't worry." Lexy picked at the paper on her muffin and avoided eye contact. "We've talked about it. A little. He goes to church regularly. He believes in God, and wants to become more serious about his faith."

Cassie reached out and put her hand on Lexy's. "We don't mean to chastise. We just want what's best for you. We love you."

"Thanks. I love you guys, too. But I'll be okay."

"Just remember," Maggie said. "Faith has to come first. If you find out he's not serious about God, it'll be a lot harder to pull back once you give your heart to him."

"What about you?" Lexy's gaze finally connected to Cassie's. "Do you have plans with Daniel?"

Now it was Cassie's turn to stare at her muffin. "Uh… he asked, but I'm not ready."

Maggie slapped the table. "Oh, come on! Enough already! You two were born ready for each other."

"It's not that simple."

"Uh, yeah it is! He loves you. You love him. You both love God. Hello?"

"Yup," Lexy chimed in. "Simple."

Cassie shook her head. "I've never said I love him. And there's more to it. What about Spencer?"

"What about him? Do you still love him?" Maggie asked.

"I never did. And that's part of the problem. I barged ahead of God and ended up hurting Spencer in the long run. And Daniel, while he watched what I was doing."

"And yet he's still here," Lexy added. "Waiting for you."

"Exactly." Maggie turned her cup on its saucer. "He forgave you, so you should forgive yourself."

"But what if I'm running ahead of God again? I couldn't bear it if I messed things up with Daniel."

"Maybe you're messing it up by stalling." Lexy tilted her head. "Or maybe, you're just scared."

"Are you scared, Cassie?" Maggie asked softly.

"I'm not afraid, but I don't want to hurt him. I don't want to rush ahead of God. And I don't want to mess this up and… and… risk losing him."

Both Maggie and Lexy grinned.

"So, you *do* want to be with him." Lexy winked.

"I… can we talk about something else?" Cassie didn't want to spend any more time thinking about the feelings she may or may not have for Daniel. She looked at her sister-in-law. "Is my brother doing anything nice for you, Maggie?"

"Rick's taking me to the Blackhorse Inn. We're having dinner and staying the night. Grams is taking the girls overnight."

"The Blackhorse!" Lexy gasped. "I've heard their Valentine's wine list is to die for!"

"I won't be having any wine."

"Why not?" Cassie asked. "Too expensive?"

"That and... other reasons." Maggie rubbed her belly.

"What? Are you?"

Maggie nodded.

Cassie squealed and clasped her mouth with both hands. Then joined Lexy in rushing around the table to give Maggie a hug.

"Congratulations!" Cassie gushed. "When are you due?"

"It's early days. We really weren't going to tell anyone yet, but I couldn't resist telling you two."

"Does Grams know?"

"Yes. But only since last night."

"So exciting!" Lexy returned to her seat. "What do the girls think?"

"We're waiting a bit longer before we tell them. Just to be sure."

Cassie sat. "I get to be an aunt—again! Yay!"

Maggie laughed. "And I'll have another child spoiled by their loving aunt."

"Always."

"Oh—so is this a good time to mention I might need some time off in a few months?"

"Sorry." Cassie shook her head. "You'll have to

bring the baby with you to the store."

The girls laughed.

"Speaking of which." Lexy checked her phone. "It's almost time to get going. And I still need to tell you the latest news about Marilyn Howard."

"Oh?" Cassie gulped down the last piece of her breakfast. "What did you find out?"

"I spent some time at the Land Registry office yesterday checking out the neighbouring houses. Turns out two of those houses are still occupied by the same people as in 1968."

"Really? Who?"

Lexy smirked. "The first is our favourite friend, Edward Morris."

"Oh no."

"Is he the old guy who threatened to call the cops on you?" Maggie asked.

"Yes." Cassie groaned. "Who's the other?"

Lexy tapped her phone and read, "Charles Whitehorn. He lives in the house next to the mansion, on the north side."

"Oh, goody!" Cassie clapped her hands. "Is Brent going to interview them?"

"Yes, but not until this afternoon."

"Hmm…" Cassie turned to Maggie. "Are you working for Rick this morning before you come to the store?"

"No… why?"

"Feel like starting a bit early so I can run a couple

of errands?"

Maggie lowered her stare. "What *kind* of errands would those be, Cassie?"

"Nothing crazy. I think it might be time for Anna to meet her new neighbours. I might go with her to make sure she doesn't slip and fall on the icy sidewalks."

Lexy frowned. "I have nothing to do with this. I promised Brent I'd stop being sneaky with you about the cases."

"But you just told me the names of the neighbours who might be witnesses or suspects, didn't you?"

Lexy nodded. "But Brent said I could. He never said anything about you visiting them."

"Hmm…" Maggie frowned.

"What are you thinking?" Cassie asked.

"That you need to be careful. Don't step on Brent's toes."

Cassie thought a moment. Was she crossing a line again? No. Of course not. She wasn't going to interview the neighbours—not directly, anyway. She was only going to visit. In fact, she might be more successful in retrieving information from them than a cop would. Especially if they knew something.

And Brent probably knew that.

Essentially, she'd be following through on his intent by doing this.

Wouldn't she?

Chapter 10

"I come bearing gifts!" Cassie held up three pie boxes as Anna held open the door.

"Cassie! What a nice surprise." Anna smiled as she let Cassie in.

"Are you free for a little bit?"

"Sure. Who's minding the store?

Cassie set the pies on a side table and kicked off her boots. "Maggie went in early today."

"That was nice of her." Anna rubbed her belly. "The baby's kicking like crazy this morning. I think he wants out."

"He?"

"Or she." Anna grinned. "We still don't know."

Cassie hung up her coat, grabbed the pies, and

followed Anna into the kitchen. "I love this kitchen. It's so cute!"

"We never did get to the house tour the other day. Sorry about that."

"No problem at all. You have a seat, and I'll take care of the pie. Apple, cherry, or pecan?"

"Mmm! Pecan, please." Anna ignored Cassie's direction to sit and went to get plates and forks instead. She set them beside the pies. "To what do I owe the pleasure of your visit?"

Cassie licked some crumbs from her finger. "I have a favour to ask, actually."

"I knew you'd have an ulterior motive." Anna grinned.

"The other two pies aren't for you and Zach. They're for your neighbours."

"Our neighbours? I don't follow."

"I thought it was time you introduced yourself to some people in the neighbourhood."

Anna sat at the kitchen table with her pie. "I think I see where you're going with this. Any neighbours in particular you'd like me to meet?"

"Charles Whitehorn across the street, and Edward Morris next door."

"Edward? Ugh. We've already met him. A few times." Anna took a big bite of pecans.

"So have I. But it turns out he, and Charles, were both living here in 1968 when the murder happened. If they have any information, I'd love to hear it." Cassie found a glass and poured herself some water from the purifying jug on the counter. "Water?"

"Yes, please. You're telling me Edward and Charles both knew the victim?"

"Uh-huh. And her husband, Wayne."

Anna gulped as she swallowed a bite of pie. "Wait. How do you know one of them didn't murder her?"

"I was hoping you wouldn't think about that." Cassie gave Anna a sheepish grin as she delivered the water to the table and took a seat. "It's a possibility."

"Great. Nice street we picked. Now my neighbours include a ghost and a murderer. Who next?"

"Don't worry. It's likely the murderer isn't either of your neighbours."

"I'm not so sure. If looks could kill, Edward's already murdered Zach and me a hundred times over."

Cassie used the side of her fork to cut into her pie. "I'm sorry. Forget I asked. It was wrong of me to ask you to do this—especially in your condition."

Anna laughed. "My *condition?* Oh, Cassie, I've told you before. I'm pregnant, not sick. And I'm just being silly. Of course I'll take you to meet the neighbours. I know this is important to you."

"Thank you." Cassie let out a breath.

"I'd visit with a thousand murderers if it helped you, my friend. Especially after all you've done for Zach and me."

"You don't owe me anything. It was my pleasure to help you both."

Anna smiled and downed her last bite. "Who do you want to start with?"

"Charles, I think." Cassie sliced her own remaining bit of pie into two pieces. "I'm not keen on chatting with Edward."

"Who knows? Maybe he'll be friendly. We've never brought him pie before."

Cassie laughed as she finished her treat and brought her dishes to the sink. She picked up the apple pie and followed Anna back out to the foyer, where she helped her friend step into her boots and get her coat zipped around her large belly.

"This is ridiculous!" Anna laughed as the zipper stuck. "And I've still got two weeks to go!"

"I bet you're excited to see this little guy face-to-face."

"We can't wait."

Cassie held the door for Anna and followed her down the walkway.

"Which house is it?" Anna asked.

Cassie pointed to a small bungalow with overgrown shrubs and worn siding. Plastic covered the windows. She assumed it was to keep the heat in for winter, but by the looks of the trees growing over the edges, the plastic had been there for a long time.

Anna frowned and crossed the street. "I hope he's home."

"Let's find out."

Cassie held Anna's arm as they made their way up

the snowy walkway. It hadn't been shovelled recently, but the snow had been tramped down from someone walking on it. Cassie pushed the round doorbell button, but it didn't light up, and she didn't hear it ring. She opted to knock loudly on the door instead.

"Who is it?" A rough voice called through the door.

"It's your new neighbour. My name is Anna."

The door opened a crack, and a bald-headed man peeked through the opening. "Are you the gal from across the street?"

Anna nodded. "Yes."

"We brought pie." Cassie held up the box.

Charles eyed Cassie up and down. "And who are you?"

"This is my friend, Cassie Bridgestone," Anna answered. "Can we come in for a minute? It's cold out here."

Charles looked at Anna's protruding belly and pulled the door open wide. "Sure. Right this way."

After removing their boots and coats, they followed Charles into a sparsely decorated living room. Old paint-by-number paintings hung on the wall, and a television cabinet displayed an old flatscreen, a few toppled books, a duck decoy, a bowling trophy, and a messy stack of papers and bills. The two brown couches were old and faded, looking as if they'd been here since 1968, too. "I hope you like apple." Cassie held out the pie.

"Yes, thank you. Would you like some?"

"Why don't you save it for yourself." Anna grinned at Cassie and whispered as Charles carried the pie into the kitchen, "Maybe we shouldn't have eaten the pecan!"

"Yeah, I wasn't thinking about having pie in three places!"

"You like your new house?" Charles returned and sat on the nearest sofa, indicating with a wave of his hand that the girls should sit on the other.

"We do. And it's a lovely street." Anna sat.

Cassie felt a spring dig into her backside as she settled beside Anna. "And I love the house next door!" She nodded in the direction of the mansion. "What do you know about it?"

Charles' eyes narrowed. "That old place? It needs to be torn down."

"The police were there the other day." Anna lowered her voice as if someone might overhear. "I heard they found a body."

"Did they?" He turned to Cassie. "What's your name, miss?"

"Cassie. I own the Olde Crow Primitives shop on Main."

"Oh." Charles got up and went to the kitchen. "There's some pie in here, would you girls like any?"

Anna and Cassie exchanged confused glances. "No, thank you," Cassie answered.

Charles returned to his seat. "It's nice to meet you. I'm Charles. What can I help you with?"

"I just wanted to introduce myself," Anna said. "I'd like to get to know all my new neighbours."

"There's a new couple moved in across the street."

"Yes, that's me."

"Oh." Charles stared at the floor and then looked up at Cassie. "And what's your name?"

"Cassie."

"Can I get you girls anything?" He stood and walked to the kitchen. "There's some pie in here."

Cassie sighed. Clearly, Charles wasn't going to be able to help them. Unless only his short-term memory was affected. "Mr. Whitehorn?"

Charles popped back into the living room. "Yes?"

"Have you lived here long?"

"Oh, yes. I moved here in… in…" He furrowed his brows. "A long time ago."

Time to cut to the chase. "Did you ever meet the people who lived in the house next door?"

"The mansion?"

Cassie nodded.

Charles looked out the picture window and to the street. Cassie followed his gaze. The plastic let light in, but the view was obscured. She could make out the shapes of houses and cars, but that was about it.

A moment later, Charles looked back at the girls. "I'm Charles. Who are you girls?"

Cassie stood and helped Anna to her feet. "Time to go, I think."

Anna frowned and nodded.

"Would you like something to eat?" Charles asked them.

"No thank you, Mr. Whitehorn," Anna answered. "We should be going now."

"Come back again." He followed them to the door.

Cassie shoved her boots on and again helped direct Anna's feet into hers. Then they slipped on their coats.

"Thank you for the visit, Charles." Cassie smiled. "It was nice to meet you."

"What's your name?"

"Cassie. And this is Anna, your new neighbour."

He smiled and squinted as he winked both eyes. "Nice to meet you, dear." He grabbed her hand and shook it with both of his.

"Nice to meet you. Enjoy your pie, Mr. Whitehorn."

Anna waddled back across the street with Cassie by her side. "Poor, old man."

Cassie shook her head. "How long do you think he's been like that?"

"Not sure. But it can't be safe for him to be living alone."

"Do you think anyone checks on him?"

"If not, Zach and I will be."

Cassie sighed as she opened Anna's front door. "Do you think he eats okay?"

"No idea. He looks healthy enough."

"And the house was warm, so that's something. Brent is heading over there later today. I'll see what he says." Cassie stepped out of her boots. "Stay here. I'll get the pie for Edward."

"But I have to pee!"

Cassie laughed. "Fine. But make it quick." She helped Anna pull her boots off.

"I must admit, I'm liking the service."

"I'm just afraid if you fall over, you might roll away."

"On second thought, I'm feeling a bit tired. Maybe we should postpone our visit to Edward?" Anna feigned a yawn.

"What I meant was, I'm glad to help you. I love putting your swollen feet into your boots for you."

Anna giggled. "That's what I thought."

Chapter 11

Cassie balanced the cherry pie in one hand and closed Anna's door behind her. She looked over at Edward's house on the other side of the hedge. The car was in the driveway, so he was bound to be home.

"Are you sure you want to do this?" Anna tugged on her coat, trying to pull the zipper up over her belly.

"I need to. He might be able to help."

"I don't think helping people is one of his strengths." Anna frowned. "The other day, I was bringing a bag of groceries in and dropped it on the driveway. He was shovelling his front step and watched the whole time while I struggled to pick things up."

"He didn't help you?" Cassie huffed. "You could

have fallen and maybe even have hurt the baby."

"Yup. He did yell at me, though, wanting to make sure I didn't leave any garbage laying around."

"Awful." Cassie shook her head but then remembered how God calls His followers to show love to everyone. "Maybe he's just lonely and needs a friend."

"Or maybe he's just a mean, old man." Anna stepped onto Edward's walkway.

"One way or the other, we're about to find out."

Cassie reached the door ahead of Anna and knocked. No one answered. She knocked again.

"Go away!" Edward's snarly voice yelled through the door.

"Mr. Morris?" Cassie called. "We have a pie for you."

"I said, go away! I'm not buying nothin'."

"We're not trying to sell you anything. It's a gift. It's free."

The door opened a crack and his bulbous nose poked through. "What's the catch?"

"No catch, Mr. Morris." Anna peered around Cassie's shoulder. "Just being a friendly neighbour."

"Fine." He opened the door, snatched the pie, and proceeded to push the door shut again.

But not before Cassie wedged her toe between the door and the jamb.

"Hey." Edward pulled the door open again.

Cassie took the opportunity to step into the house,

pulling Anna in behind her. "My name is Cassie, and this is your new neighbour, Anna."

Anna held out her hand. "It's nice to officially meet you."

Edward sneered but backed away. "Close the door then. I'm not paying to heat the outside." He turned and walked through the living room, taking the pie with him.

"That was bold," Anna whispered.

"Yes, but it worked! Hurry. Get your boots and coat off before he kicks us out." Cassie helped her friend out of her winter garb and led her to an old recliner to sit. The mixed scent of mustiness, pipe tobacco, and body odour filled the air.

The room was dated, with old panelling on the walls, a thick carpet, and worn, fabric couches. Apparently, Charles and Edward had used the same decorator. Unlike Charles' home, however, Edward's was full of clutter. Stacks of old newspapers sat on the end of one of the couches. Clothes were strewn about, old takeout containers covered the coffee table, and the shelves were stuffed full of trinkets and model antique cars.

Edward returned from the kitchen, without the pie or any plates. Clearly, his lack of hospitality extended beyond absent invites.

He stopped in front of Anna. "That's my chair."

Cassie resisted the urge to sigh, or worse—say something she'd regret. Instead, she arose to help Anna out of the chair and over to the couch. Anna glared at her when Edward wasn't looking.

"You have a lovely home," Cassie forced the words out. "How long have you lived here?"

"I've always lived here."

"You were born in this house?"

"Of course not. I meant since I was on my own."

Anna shifted, trying to get comfortable. "Were you married?"

"Yup. Bernice died in eighty-three. Didn't even ask permission."

Cassie wasn't sure if he was serious or not. "Do you have children?"

"Nope. Never had no use for the little brats."

Anna put her hand on her stomach as if creating a shield between Edward and the baby.

Cassie patted Anna's hand and turned back to the cantankerous old man. "If you've been here that long, you must remember the couple who used to live in the mansion across the street."

"That's where I've seen you." He slapped the arm of the chair. "You were one of them folks who broke in a few days ago."

"Uh, yes. I was there," Cassie said. "It must have been a beautiful home in its day."

Edward grabbed a pipe and a match from the adjacent side table. "Yup. T'was."

As he proceeded to light his pipe, Cassie knew her time was short. There was no way Anna was going to stick around in the smoky air. Nor should she. "Can you tell us about Marilyn and Wayne?"

"Not much to say."

Anna coughed as Edward puffed his pipe and small clouds of smoke infiltrated the air.

"What happened when they left?" Cassie asked.

"Dunno. One day, they just up and went. Never saw 'em again. Though if she was swinging from the attic rafters, that would explain why."

Anna emitted a small gasp and covered her mouth.

Cassie grimaced. How could someone be so crass and uncompassionate? What had happened in his life to make him so callous? "Did you know her at all? Before then?"

"Nope. Saw her in her gardens sometimes. Leaving piles of weeds on her lawn for the whole street to see. And sometimes she rang up my groceries at Boersley's."

"She worked at the grocery store?" Cassie thought of the little grocery market on Main Street. It had been around for years, offering staples to the community.

"Yup. Don't know why. That husband of hers was loaded. Guess she was one of them types that actually likes people."

Anna coughed again and touched Cassie's arm. The smoke in the room thickened. "Cassie…"

Cassie nodded. "I know. Okay." She turned to Edward and stood. "Thank you for the visit, but we must be going now."

"Make sure you shut the door tight on your way out." He puffed his pipe again and reclined his chair, causing Anna to have to step around him.

Cassie and Anna redressed into their outwear as quickly as possible and stepped out into the chilly air, shutting Edward into the smoky house behind them.

Anna took a deep breath. "I can breathe!"

"Yes. Edward's not exactly a breath of fresh air, is he?"

"No. And I don't care if I ever talk to him again. Did you see him? He lit up that pipe with no concern for the baby. Or us!"

"I'm sorry. We should've left right away." Cassie took Anna's arm as she stepped onto the curb to get around the hedge.

"I was going to ask him to put it out, but I knew there'd be no point. I only wish he'd had more helpful information for you. At least the visit would have been worth it, then."

"I'm disappointed, yes." The snow crunched under Cassie's feet as she walked up Zach's and Anna's driveway. "I thought I'd learn a lot more this morning. But I'm not leaving entirely empty-handed."

"What do you mean? What did I miss?"

"First of all, Marilyn worked at the grocery store. I might be able to find someone who worked with her at Boersley's. Maybe even someone who she'd confided in."

Anna shivered as she started up her front walk. "And second?"

"I'm not sure yet, but think about this. We just

spent time with a man who hates people, is always annoyed at something, and has no regard for anyone around him."

Anna gasped and turned back to Cassie. "You think...?"

"I don't know. But those are certainly the type of qualities I'd expect in a murderer."

"Hey!" Anna pointed at the mansion. "Look."

Cassie whirled around to stare at the cold, empty building. It was quiet, and still. "What am I looking at?"

"Oh, nothing." Anna waved her hand and reached for her doorhandle.

"What? What did you see, Anna?"

She looked past Cassie, her face paler than it should be in the cold winter air. "Upstairs. By the second window. I saw a shadow move in front of it."

Cassie looked over her shoulder at the house, but it was still quiet. And there was no movement behind any of the windows that weren't boarded up. "I think you need to sit down. I pushed you to do too much this morning."

"You're right." Anna pushed the door open. "I must be imagining things."

And yet Cassie watched Anna give one more glance at the house, her eyes wide and lips pressed together.

Chapter 12

"Can we please get a BeaverTail, Mom?" Eleven-year-old Olivia poked Maggie with her fluffy mitten as Maggie tied her daughter's skates.

"Yeah!" The younger Lily chimed in. "Please?"

"BeaverTail? What's that?" Daniel skated up beside Cassie.

"For real?" Cassie pulled her toque down to her brows. "You've never skated on the Rideau Canal, and now you're telling me you've never had a BeaverTail, either? You've been seriously deprived."

"So, educate me."

"You'll have to catch me, first." Cassie quickly skated away from the bench, with Daniel at her heels.

She was glad Maggie and Rick had asked them to join in on an evening skate up the canal in Ottawa. It had been a slow day at Olde Crow Primitives, and all day long, her mind had been mulling over the murder and lack of information. She'd grown a whole new level of respect for those who toiled over cold cases.

"Ha!" Daniel grabbed her around the waist. "Gotcha."

Cassie giggled and pretended to struggle in Daniel's arms. She whirled around, and their eyes met. The reflection of a nearby streetlight made Daniel's glisten.

He held her for a moment, then let her go. "What time are we meeting Lexy and Brent?"

"A little after seven, I think." She glided alongside him back to Rick, Maggie, and the girls. "Up by the ice sculptures."

"I've heard about those famous ice sculptures. Word travels, even to Toronto."

"They're amazing. Wait until you see them!"

"There you are." Rick skated up. "The girls are all laced up. Ready to go?"

"As long as you promise to get me one of those BeaverTail things." Daniel grinned.

"Deal."

Maggie arrived and handed Rick the large backpack holding their boots while Daniel skated back to the bench to get the bag with his and Cassie's.

Moments later, the group skated up the canal. It was lower than street level, with large block walls and stairs leading up every few hundred feet. The streetlights shone down from both sides of the canal, illuminating the ice and the dozens of people on it. Everyone, young and old, seemed to be enjoying a skate on the brisk night. Couples held hands, parents towed kids on sleds, and the occasional speedskater whizzed by, darting around and between the others.

"This is great." Daniel skated up to Cassie's side. "Do you come here every year?"

"Usually a few times each winter, if the weather allows."

Daniel looked at the winding street, following alongside the canal. A few people came down a flight of stairs with skates hanging around their necks. "I know Ottawa is a city too, but it's so different than Toronto."

"Night and day. Toronto is all hustle and bustle, while Ottawa is more slow-paced and family-oriented. Except for downtown. There it's all about politics."

"You know, I've lived in Banford for almost seven months, and I still haven't visited the Parliament Buildings."

"I'll have to take you. The architecture is stunning."

"I'd like that." Daniel smiled and reached for her hand, but then stopped and pulled back.

Cassie pretended not to notice. She longed for his touch. It would be romantic—skating on the canal, holding hands. But it wasn't time. Hopefully, it would be, someday.

"Aunt Cassie!" Lily skated up, her blonde braids

hanging beneath her red *Canada* toque.

"Yes, honey?"

"Can I hold your hand while we skate?"

Cassie's heart warmed. "Of course!" She grabbed the child's mittened hand in her own. God was good, understanding, and full of mercy. If she couldn't hold Daniel's hand, God had provided her with the next best thing.

"Woah! Look at those skates!" Daniel pointed at Lily's adjustable, pink princess skates. "Did you know those skates have special powers?"

"Really?" Lily almost lost her footing as she gazed at Daniel with big eyes.

"Yup." Daniel leaned in and spoke behind his hand in a big whisper. "They can make you fly."

"No way!"

"Yes, way! Wanna see?"

Lily nodded, making the pompom on her toque shake about.

Daniel skated to the other side of Lily and took her other hand. "But you have to hang on tight, or it won't work, okay?"

"Okay!"

Cassie noted a wink from Daniel as Lily tightened her grip on Cassie's hand.

"Ready?" Daniel picked up speed, taking Lily and Cassie with him. "1... 2... 3!"

Cassie took his cue and joined him in lifting Lily into the air.

"Whee!"

They set her down.

"Again! Again!"

After a few more flights, Olivia skated over. "My turn! My turn!"

"And then me!" Rick chimed in.

They laughed and continued to joke and have fun all the way to the ice sculpture lot. There, Cassie followed Daniel to an empty bench to remove their skates, while Rick and Maggie helped the girls.

"Wow." Daniel pulled off his gloves and rubbed his thigh. "I'm going to feel this tomorrow."

"And likely the day after that." Cassie grinned. "But it's worth it."

"Any time spent with you is worth it." He looked into her eyes and gently grazed the bottom of her chin with his cold finger.

A warm sensation travelled through Cassie's body.

"There you are!" Lexy's voice pierced the air. Cassie turned to see her waving from behind a low iron fence at the edge of the canal. Brent had his arm around her.

Cassie waved and finished removing her skates. Then she tied the ends of the laces together and hung the skates around their neck.

Lexy met her at the top of the stairs and gave her a hug. "Having fun?" She eyed Daniel as he shook Brent's hand.

"Yes. How about you?" Cassie did her own eyeing as she looked at Brent's free hand, reaching for Lexy's.

She smiled and mouthed, "Best night ever."

When the others caught up, the group made their way over to the ice sculptures.

"This is incredible!" Daniel took out his phone to snap a few photos of two ice stallions galloping in the snow.

"Look at this one, Mr. Daniel!" Lily tugged at his sleeve and directed his attention to an ice princess lying on a bed of ice flowers.

Cassie grinned, enjoying Daniel's reactions to the sculptures as much as she enjoyed the sculptures themselves. The group wound past the wonderful creations, taking in dragons, castles, lions, dolphins, and even an ice library with sculped books on all the shelves. Daniel liked that one the best.

When the tour was over, Olivia and Lily ran up to a BeaverTail kiosk to claim a place in line.

"I guess it's time for a snack." Maggie laughed.

Daniel pulled Cassie into the line and clasped his hands together. "I'm up for that."

Brent and Lexy took their spot behind them.

"What kind do you want?" Brent leaned in close to Lexy, attentively waiting for her answer.

"The chocolate banana one."

"What?" Daniel furrowed his brows. "What are these things?" He looked at a couple of people heading away from the kiosk, their BeaverTails in hand.

"The most delectable pastries you'll ever have." Cassie hugged herself and grinned. "They're long and flat, like a beaver's tail, and covered in cinnamon, sugar, or specialty toppings like chocolate or brownies."

"Just remember," Rick jabbed Daniel's shoulder. "I only offered to pay for *one*."

Fifteen minutes later, the group gathered at a nearby tree to enjoy their delicacies. Cassie savoured every bit of each bite—both chewy and crunchy at the same time.

"These... these are...mmm..." Daniel took another bite before he could finish his sentence.

Brent stole a bite of Lexy's. "My sentiments exactly. I'm glad I didn't have to work tonight."

"Speaking of work..." Cassie found her way in. "How did the interviews with the neighbours go today?"

"A waste of time. One guy tried to refuse us entry, and after he relented, he refused to answer my questions. Was upset we'd allowed a murder to take place on his street."

Cassie knew this must have been Edward Morris. "Did you explain to him you weren't on the force then?" She giggled.

"Yup. He didn't seem to care."

"And the other neighbour?"

Brent shook his head. "No help. He has dementia and could barely carry a conversation."

"I see. Is he safe living alone?"

"How do you know he lives alone?" He glanced at Lexy, who only shrugged.

"I visited with Anna today." And her neighbours,

but she wasn't about to tell Brent that—yet.

"Hmm." Brent studied her as if waiting for more information.

Cassie stayed silent.

He continued. "We're sending someone to check in on him next week. To try and get him a proper assessment."

"Good. I'm glad. And I know Anna will be, too. Did you find out anything interesting at all?"

"Oh!" Lexy elbowed Brent between bites. "Tell her about Edward's call!"

"Call?" Cassie watched Brent's face. It held a normal expression, so he must not have minded Lexy mentioning it.

"He called just as we were leaving to come here, to make a complaint about noise coming from the mansion."

"Noise? What kind of noise?"

"A screeching, wailing noise. Says he hasn't heard it since the seventies. Figures by moving the remains, we upset the ghost who lives there."

"Interesting." Cassie ran her fingers over her mouth.

"Why?"

"Anna swore she saw shadows moving in front of the upstairs windows of the mansion this morning."

"She saw the ghost?" Lexy crumpled up her empty BeaverTail wrapper.

"I didn't say she saw a ghost," Cassie answered.

"But she did see a shadow. Something's going on in there."

"And *I* will find out what it is." Brent cast Cassie a warning glare.

Cassie smiled and nodded, but a plan already started to form in her mind. She'd agreed not to break anymore laws or act unethically, but that didn't mean she couldn't snoop within certain boundaries.

Chapter 13

Despite the soreness in her legs from skating the night before, Cassie decided to treat herself to a brisk walk before opening the store. The air was cool but refreshing. There were no sounds except the crisp snow under her feet and the chorus of chickadees and blue jays visiting various shrubs for their breakfast.

Though the mergansers swimming in the mist beyond the ice were breathtaking, her quick jaunt down the river path didn't turn up any eagles. She'd have to make more of an effort to check for them regularly. Cassie turned back to the street to walk the quaint village blocks instead.

A few people were out and about, filling their bird feeders or starting up their cars, but most of the sleepytown villagers seemed to be taking comfort inside their warm, cozy homes. Including those on Elm Street.

Cassie couldn't help herself. She had to walk by the mansion. It was still and quiet, as usual, but for some reason, Cassie felt like the air thickened as she neared— as if there was a tension surrounding it.

Or maybe she was feeling her own anxiety. For years and years, her dream mansion had housed a murdered woman in its rafters. Who could have done such a thing? And why? The unanswered questions penetrated her mind without relenting.

She glanced up and down the street. No home showed any signs of life. Would anyone notice if she snuck up to the porch and peeked in a window?

Her glance lingered on Edward's home. The curtains were drawn.

Cassie rushed up the walkway to the mansion before she could change her mind. It wouldn't hurt to look, would it?

She walked around the side of the porch to the nearest non-boarded window and put her face to the glass. The panes were thin and murky, and the darkness inside made it impossible to see anything.

Cassie frowned and returned to the front of the porch. Maybe this was a silly idea. What did she expect to see? A ghost-making machine in plain sight?

Ghosts. Both Anna and Edward had seen or heard something. *Someone* had to be trying to scare people away. But why? What was still to be found in this mysterious mansion?

On a whim, Cassie tried the front door handle. Locked. Brent had greased the mechanism and got it working before the investigators arrived the other day, and had kept the key. She jiggled the handle up and down in frustration. The latch clicked.

It opened!

The police using it after all these years must have jarred the old parts loose inside.

Cassie couldn't resist. After another quick glance at Edward's closed curtains, she let herself inside.

She shivered. Was it possible the house was colder inside than out? Cassie shook her head and chalked it up to nerves.

Everything looked the same as the last time she was here. She turned on her phone's flashlight to illuminate the space.

No, things weren't quite the same.

She directed the light beam to a painting on the wall. The dust along the frame had been disturbed. Someone had touched it. Cassie gently pulled the side of the picture away from the wall, but there was nothing behind it. Then she noticed the same dust disturbance on the next painting. And the one after that. And inside the grand piano and on the end table. In fact, everything in the room had been touched or moved and put back. Her neck muscles tensed.

But then, Cassie recalled the number of people who'd been in the house when the forensics team had been here to do their duty. Of course. They'd probably given the place a good going over as part of their investigation. Her shoulders relaxed a little.

She thought of the crime scene. There had been so many crates and boxes in the attic. Did the investigators go through everything? Was it all strewn about? What was in all those boxes, anyway? Again, an irresistible urge drew her forth. She was already inside the house. What would it hurt to peek upstairs? Perhaps she could discover something the investigators had missed, and get back on Brent's good side. Besides, the successes she'd had at solving mysteries over the last year increased her thirst for righting wrongs. And thinking of poor Marilyn, alone in this mansion without justice being served... Cassie chewed her lip. It was unfair and something had to be done about it.

Cassie quietly climbed the sweeping staircase to the second floor, momentarily imagining Marilyn in her cute sixties dress, descending the same stairs. What had really happened to her? Did her husband really murder her? Had Edward? And if it was someone else, who? And why?

The second floor had been equally gone over by the forensics team. Some of the peeling wallpaper had been ripped off and lay in a heap on the floor. A painting had been completely removed and sat leaning against the wall in the hall. She peeked into a bedroom. The old quilt and blankets had been pulled off the bed, and the mattress tipped onto its side.

Creak. Thump.

Noises came from one of the other bedrooms. Cassie peeked around her room's doorway and into the hall.

It was quiet again.

Which room had the noise come from? She tiptoed down the hall and peeked into the next bedroom. Empty.

Thump.

Cassie jerked her head toward the room at the end. Someone, or *something*, was in there.

She shook her head. It wasn't some*thing*. It was some*one*. But who?

Stealthily, Cassie moved down the hallway. Until a board creaked under her feet.

Another *thump*. And then silence.

Against her better judgement, Cassie ran into the room, shining her flashlight into its corners.

Nothing.

No one.

She turned. If someone was here, the closet was the only place to hide. Her mind screamed at her. She should leave. Now. If there really was someone hiding there, what motive would they have? Was it someone connected to the murder? Someone with information? On the other hand, did she really want to confront someone in a big, empty house?

Yet, if someone could share further details about the murder, wouldn't she be helping Brent by finding out?

Another thought struck her. Maybe the person in there *was* the murderer. If so, Cassie could solve the case right now.

To be safe, Cassie lifted her phone and scrolled to the page where she had Daniel's number on speed dial. Her thumb hovered over the photo, ready to tap in an instant if necessary.

Holding her breath, Cassie reached for the closet doorknob. This was it. The moment of truth. Before she could chicken out, she yanked the door open and directed her light into the darkness.

Empty.

This made no sense. She'd heard someone in this room. She pushed some clothing aside to double check behind the long dresses.

Nothing.

Cassie pushed on the back of the closet to see if the wall would give. Could there be a secret passage?

But the wall was solid.

She sighed and turned to examine each wall of the bedroom. Other than some torn paper and graffiti, nothing seemed abnormal. There were no odd creases in the wall or bookcases to move.

Could she have been wrong about which room the noise originated from?

Cassie scurried back into the hallway and quickly scanned the other three rooms.

No one was here.

A sudden scratching noise above her made her jump. The attic.

She aimed her light up and followed the noise across the ceiling and down the wall.

Cassie laughed. It must be a squirrel! She shook her head and sighed. All this talk of ghost stories and she, herself, had been taken in. How ridiculous.

She checked her phone. It was time to head home and get ready for work. Still laughing at her foolishness, Cassie skipped down the stairs to the main floor, sliding her hand along the dusty banister rail.

At the bottom, she followed the railing as it curved and brought her to the side table where Daniel had found Marilyn's photo. There was another photo there, jammed between the wall and the table. Cassie pulled it out of the crack and dusted it off. A man wearing a polyester suit stared back at her. He had similar features to Wayne Howard. Maybe a photo of him as a young man.

Again, she mulled over the mystery. What had happened all those years ago? Would they ever find the truth this many years later?

Something whizzed by her head.

Smash!

An old porcelain vase lay in pieces on the floor, inches away from her.

"Hey!" Cassie yelled up the stairs. "I know you're up there! Who are you?"

Her call was met with silence.

She inched toward the front door, keeping her eye on the stairs, and pulled Brent's number up on her phone.

"Cassie? What's up?"

"Brent! I'm at the mansion. I think someone just tried to kill me."

Chapter 14

"Get out of there, now!" Brent commanded. "I'll be right over. Promise me you'll leave."

"I will. I promise. Leaving now." Cassie reached behind her to open the door, keeping an eye on the stairs the entire time.

"Are you hurt at all?"

"No."

"Thank God. Wait for us out on the sidewalk. And if someone comes out of the house, run away. I *mean* it!"

"Okay, okay. I will."

Cassie shut the door behind her and ran down the porch steps. Brent was angry with her. And rightfully so. But if he caught the killer, Cassie was sure he'd forgive her.

She walked backwards down the walkway, keeping an eye on the front door. If anyone ran out of the house, she'd see who it was. She held her phone up, ready to snap a photo.

A siren wailed. Brent was already on the way. Thankfully the station was only a couple of blocks over—another benefit of a small town.

The siren stopped, but lights flashed as the police car pulled onto Elm Street. Cassie quickly redirected her gaze back to the house. No way was she going to miss someone coming out.

The car stopped behind her, and two car doors slammed.

Lexy ran up. "Cassie! Are you okay?"

"I'm fine."

"What happened?" Brent appeared, dressed head to toe in his black police garb.

"Someone threw a vase at my head. But they missed. I'm all right."

He gently grabbed her arm. "What were you doing in there? You can't keep overstepping me, Cassie. You're going to get yourself killed!"

"I'm sorry! I didn't mean to. I was walking by and… I couldn't resist taking a peek."

"Well, you're going to have to learn how to resist. From now on. Or the only thing you'll end up having a chance to resist is an arrest."

"Okay. I get it." Cassie frowned. "But in the

meantime, the culprit is in the house. I'm sure they either know about the murder, or are directly involved."

Brent squinted as he studied Cassie's face. Then he sighed and ran up the walkway. "Stay there," he called.

Lexy wrapped her arms around Cassie. "You look cold."

"I'm freezing." Cassie shivered. "How angry was he?"

"Pretty angry."

"At least I didn't get you caught in the middle this time."

Lexy let go. "No, but it would've directly affected me if you'd gotten hurt. It's not only your own life you're messing with, you know."

"I know. I'm sorry! I don't mean to—"

"But you're using the mystery to silence everything else going on in your mind."

Cassie furrowed her brows. "What do you mean?"

"I mean, you like adventure. And I think you're afraid and avoiding a potential adventure with Daniel. So, you're trying to fill the void with a different adventure instead."

"That's ridiculous." Cassie waved her hand. "I want to help, that's all. I feel for this poor woman. My mind has romanticized this house and its history for so many years; I just want to set it right. And I'm *not* afraid of a relationship with Daniel. And one has nothing to do with the other."

"Mm-hmm." Lexy put her hand on her hip. "Sure."

The girls stood in silence until the front door slammed. "No one's in there, Cassie." Brent jogged down the steps.

"Are you sure? There has to be. Did you check the attic? There are lots of places to hide."

"I'm sure. But since you're here, let's go in and take another look around. Show me exactly what happened."

The girls followed Brent back into the house as Cassie explained the incident.

"The front door lock just broke?" Brent asked. "Are you sure you didn't *help* it?

"Honest." Cassie held her hand up as if swearing an oath. "I only jiggled it. And once I was inside, I noticed the investigators had touched everything in the house, and I got curious. I wanted to see what was in the attic. When I got to the second floor, I heard a noise and went into the bedroom to see what it was."

Lexy swatted Cassie's arm. "You went *to* the noise? Are you nuts?"

Cassie shrugged. "But there was no one there. And when I heard a squirrel skitter across the hall inside the ceiling, I figured that was the noise I'd heard. But when I went downstairs, someone threw that vase at my head." She pointed to the remnants.

Brent moved a few pieces with the toe of his boot. "Are you sure you didn't bump the table and knock it down?"

"Positive. I saw it whiz past my head."

"Maybe the squirrel knocked it down?" Lexy gazed

up the stairs, wide-eyed.

"Or maybe it was the ghost, right?" Cassie scoffed. "Is that what you really want to say?"

"Of course not." Lexy stepped closer to Brent.

"Let's take another look." He directed his flashlight up the stairs.

The girls followed Brent to the second floor, where he proceeded to examine the hallway. "There's no table here the vase could have fallen from."

"See?"

"Let's do another thorough search. But stay with me."

Brent went downstairs to start on the ground floor. Cassie and Lexy followed closely behind, helping him search closets and large furniture for any possible hiding place he might have missed his first time through. They paused at the back door, taking a moment to double-check the mound of snow blown up against it. No one had used this door in a long time.

A small door in the kitchen led to a crawl space under the house. The girls followed him down the shaky wooden staircase and waited at the bottom while Brent hunched over to walk around. The room was mostly empty, save for a few old crates, and only took moments to search. Then they headed back up to the second floor, checked every room and closet, and finally went up to the attic.

Cassie gasped. All the crates and trunks had been opened, and their contents were strewn about. Before, it was difficult to get around. Now it was near impossible. "Wow, this is crazy! Did the forensics team do this?"

"Definitely not. They would never be so disrespectful." Lexy hugged herself and shivered. "It certainly wasn't like this when we left."

Brent nodded. "I didn't want to say anything earlier, but Lexy's right. All the things and paintings that you noticed had been touched? That wasn't from us."

"Then there *is* someone in here. Or at least there was." Cassie rubbed her chin. "And that someone is looking for something."

"Likely something which ties them to the murder," Brent added.

Cassie gasped. "So, it *was* Marilyn's killer in here with me?"

"Looks that way."

"Do you think they found whatever they were looking for?" Lexy's eyes darted around the room.

"No." Cassie shook her head. "If they had, they wouldn't still have been here when I showed up."

"Lexy, call head office. We're going to need another team here." Brent stepped over a pile of old clothes. "I'm going to do one more search up here while we wait."

Cassie rubbed her temples. "How did the killer get past us? Where did he go?"

"Your guess is as good as mine. But I know where you're going to go. You're going to work—at your store."

Cassie nodded. "Okay."

"And you will *not* come back to this mansion by yourself, or approach a suspect by yourself, or do *anything* that could jeopardize your safety. Do you understand?"

"But you wanted my help on the last murder case. Don't you remember? You had me spying on potential suspects."

Brent shone the flashlight directly into Cassie's eyes. "*That* was different. There were people around you at all times. Including Daniel. And that does *not* mean you can go get him to come here with you."

Cassie grinned.

"I'm serious, Cass. This isn't a joke. Someone who's gotten away with murder for this long wouldn't think twice about doing it again."

"At least they're old and feeble." Lexy kicked a crate out of her way.

"Old, yes." Brent nodded. "Feeble, maybe not. But likely also not afraid of a life sentence at their age."

Cassie gulped. "Okay. I get it. I'll pull back."

"Good. And promise me you'll come directly to me with any other information you might come across."

"I promise." Cassie thought about the fact that Marilyn had worked at Boersley's Grocery. Did that count? Brent probably knew already anyway. He would've had Marilyn's social insurance number searched and seen her places of employment.

What about Cassie's visits to Charles and Edward? It's not like she'd learned anything extra. And if she mentioned it now, it was only going to make Brent angrier. Best to leave it alone.

She sighed. The earlier conversation with Lexy ran through her mind. Was Lexy right? Was Cassie wrapping herself up in this case to avoid dealing with her feelings for Daniel? Or the breakup with Spencer? She shrugged off the notion as quickly as it had appeared. How ridiculous. A woman had been murdered. In Cassie's favourite mansion. Justice needed to be served, and Cassie would do all she could to see this mystery through.

"Cassie?" Brent raised his eyebrows at her. "What are you thinking about?"

"Nothing. Just that I have to get to work."

Chapter 15

The bells jingled as Maggie walked through the front door of Olde Crow Primitives. "I brought you a bagel."

"Thanks. I haven't eaten yet today." Cassie took the bag as Maggie whisked by on her way to the coat rack at the back.

"I figured as much."

"Rowr?" Pumpkin stood up in her bed behind the counter and stretched out her front paws.

"Aunt Maggie's here." Cassie scratched the cat under the chin, pulled the bagel out of the bag, and took a big bite.

Maggie joined Cassie behind the cash counter and rubbed Pumpkin's ears. "Have you recovered from the attack this morning?"

"It wasn't an attack. I'm perfectly fine."

Maggie raised her brows. "Not an attack? Someone tried to kill you."

"And they missed." Cassie grinned.

"I'm not smiling. You put yourself in harm's way too often, nowadays."

"But I've also helped catch several murderers."

Maggie pulled a basket of ribbon out from under the counter. Pumpkin swatted at a loose strand as it moved past her whiskers. "True. But you've had too many close calls in the process." She set the basket on the counter and placed her hands on her flat belly. "This little guy or gal wants to meet their aunt."

"And I can't wait to meet him or her." Cassie grinned and grabbed a roll of loose ribbon, pulled it tight, and worked at rewinding it.

"We're going to tell the girls this weekend."

"They'll be so excited!"

"I think so, too. Until they figure out they'll have to share a room when the baby comes."

Cassie laughed. "It'll be good for them."

"We'll see." Maggie eyed the back wall in the direction of The Book Nook. "What did Daniel have to say about your little escapade this morning?"

"I haven't told him yet."

"What? Why not? I would've thought you'd have called him before me."

Cassie shrugged. "I didn't want to worry him."

"That's ridiculous." Maggie snatched the ribbon from Cassie's hand, tossed it back in the basket, and used both hands to shove Cassie out from behind the counter and toward the back of the store. "Go see him. And take your time—I can handle the crowd."

Cassie eyed the empty store and grinned. "If you say so." She let herself out the back door and into the hallway between Olde Crow Primitives and The Book Nook but hesitated at the bookstore door.

She pondered a moment, trying to recall how many times she'd stood outside this door, thinking things through before entering. And why was she apprehensive this time? Was she anxious about upsetting him? Or was it something else?

Her mind was tired. Cassie shook her head and let herself into The Book Nook.

"Hi!" Daniel's eyes lit up like they always did when he first saw her.

Cassie wondered if hers did the same. "Time for a tea?"

Daniel looked back and forth around the store, devoid of customers. "Uh, I think I can spare a minute." He winked.

"How are your legs today?" Cassie looked down at Daniel's snug-fitting jeans and felt heat rise to her cheeks. "I mean, are you sore? From skating?" Her face had definitely turned red.

"I'm managing. You?"

"Fine. A bit sore, but not too bad. I went for a walk this morning."

Daniel walked over to the coffee bar, put a tea pod

in the machine, and shoved Cassie's favourite cat mug under the spout. "I heard."

"What do you mean?"

"Brent gave me a call earlier."

Cassie sighed and leaned her shoulder against the nearest bookshelf. "Brent has a big mouth."

"He's concerned about your safety."

"Did he ask you to babysit me or something?"

"Something like that." Daniel turned and handed Cassie her mug, a grin on his face.

She grabbed the mug and headed over to the chairs in front of the fireplace. "I'm not an irresponsible kid."

"Then maybe you should stop acting like one." Daniel sat beside her, his own coffee in hand.

"You're not being very nice," she huffed and folded her legs crisscross applesauce on the chair.

"The truth hurts sometimes."

"I'm *just* trying to solve the case."

"And we *just* care deeply about you." Daniel tucked a loose curl behind her ear.

Cassie closed her eyes at his touch and sighed. "I know. Sorry. I'm feeling a bit on edge."

"Because of this morning?"

"No. Maybe. I'm not sure." Why was she on edge? She should feel shaken up from the events of the day, but she wasn't. She hadn't been hurt, and they had another lead for the case. Brent and the other officers would be at the house all day, searching for whatever the killer had been trying to find.

Daniel continued to lean toward her. "There's frustration in your eyes. Is the case getting to you?"

"A little. But no, that's not it either." Cassie held Daniel's gaze and softened under the spell of his blue eyes. Suddenly it hit her. "It's Lexy. And Maggie. And everyone else who's pressuring me."

"Why are they pressuring you? Pressuring you into what?"

Cassie smiled at him.

"Oh," he said. "I see."

"Lexy told me I'm afraid of a relationship with you."

"Are you?"

Cassie dropped her gaze to the floor. "No. At least, I don't think so. I'm afraid of a failing relationship. One I cause to go wrong because I forged ahead of God."

"Like it did with Spencer?"

She nodded.

Daniel put his hand under her chin and directed her gaze back to him. "Did you ever think maybe it didn't work out with Spencer because he wasn't the one you were supposed to be with?"

"But that's exactly it. I misunderstood God and forged ahead. And in the process, I hurt Spencer, myself… and you."

"I'm fine." He touched his hand to his chest. "How about you? Do you still love Spencer?"

"No. Why does everyone keep asking me that? I never loved him."

"Do you still have feelings for Spencer?"

Cassie shook her head. "No. That's not it either."

"So, I'm okay—and you're okay. That's two out of three."

"And what about the third? What about Spencer? What I did to him was horrible and unfair."

Daniel's hand shifted to her knee. "Stop beating yourself up. You weren't horrible. Not at all. If you were horrible, you would've stuck with it even when you knew it wasn't right. You would have lied to him, or to yourself."

"I guess." Cassie carefully rocked her mug and watched the tea swirl back and forth. She could feel Daniel's eyes still on her.

"What else is there?"

Cassie shrugged. "I don't want to make the same mistake again."

"Moving ahead of God, you mean?"

She nodded.

"And have you talked to God about it recently?"

She picked at the handle of her mug. Had she? The last thing God had told her concerning Daniel was to *wait*. But for what? She'd waited, and he'd become a Christian. A man strong in his faith. Was she still supposed to wait?

"Cassie?"

"I don't know what to do. I don't want to rush ahead and ruin any chance of…"

"Of what, Cassie?"

She reached out and put her hand on Daniel's cheek. "I don't want to lose you." Tears welled up in her eyes.

"I'm not going anywhere." He reached across her arm and held her cheek, too.

"Then why do I feel so afraid?"

Daniel swiped one of her escaped tears with his thumb. "I don't know. But I think you should take it to God."

"And what if He doesn't answer me right away? What if it takes time, and what if—"

"I said, I'm not going anywhere." He leaned in even closer.

Cassie breathed in his scent of cinnamon and leather. She looked at his lips and the spot of stubble on his chin he'd missed while shaving.

She inched closer, and closer—

Ding. Ding.

The electric chime on the bookstore door rang as a customer entered. Daniel and Cassie both jumped a few inches in their chairs and separated before their lips could connect.

"Please. Give me a bit more time," Cassie whispered.

Daniel grabbed her hand and squeezed. "Take all the time you need." He rose and walked up to the elderly customer. "Hi. Can I help you find anything today?"

Chapter 16

Cassie pushed back a box flap and drew a set of rustic canisters labelled for coffee, tea, and flour, out of the box. She set them on the nearest display table next to a crock of aged wooden spoons and went to the cash counter to get a few price tags.

It had been another quiet morning at Olde Crow Primitives, and Cassie was grateful. Puttering around in the store gave her time to think. Not that she didn't do enough thinking as she'd tossed and turned all night, replaying the almost-kiss with Daniel in her mind and mulling over the murder case.

Lexy had called late last evening, with Brent's permission, to let Cassie know the police search at the mansion hadn't turned up anything unusual or anything that could be construed as a link to the murderer.

Cassie thought again about the vase sailing past her head. *Someone* had been in the house, and *someone* had been searching for something. How did they get by her? And Brent? The investigative team spent extra time searching for secret passageways but had come up empty. Overall, the layout didn't even allow for extra space between rooms.

What was she missing?

She fastened a price tag to the canister set with a string and dug her hands back in the box to pull out a few wooden cutting boards with handles and pictures of farm animals painted on them. She stacked them on the table, examining the space and figuring out the best way to display them. She tried standing them on their ends to make it easy to see each picture.

And then there was Daniel. What had she done? She'd almost kissed him—again. It had happened once before. Cassie silently thanked God for the customer's interruption. How could she have almost allowed a kiss to occur? And right as they were discussing her need to wait!

She shook her head. She was doing precisely the opposite of what waiting required. Overall, her behaviour had contradicted her words. It's almost as if she'd promised Daniel she *would* end up with him, as long as he was patient. But didn't that defeat the purpose of waiting? Of not barging ahead of God? She was waiting because she *wasn't* sure. And she didn't want to mess things up if he was the one God wanted her to be with.

The cutting boards toppled over like dominoes and knocked one of the metal canisters off the table. Cassie sighed and picked it up. Yup. Her life was ready to fall to pieces just like dominoes—one thing after another.

She stacked the boards into a pile as the bells on the door jingled and Grams walked in. "Hello, dear!" She placed two coffee cups from Java Junction on the counter.

Pumpkin jumped up from her hiding spot. "Rowr!"

"Hello, Pumpkin." Grams pulled off a glove to stroke the cat's back.

"Hey, Grams. Thanks for the tea."

"Thought I'd save you a trip out into the cold." She went to hang up her coat.

"Thanks. The temperature really dropped today." Cassie wrapped her hands around the warm cup. "My apartment windows were all frosted this morning."

Grams came back around the corner and tugged on the bottom of her sweater. "I don't mind too much. It's nice to get some fresh, cold air. The other residents at the manor have their heat turned way up. It's all I can do not to turn on my air conditioning."

Cassie laughed. "They're not all as fit as you, Grams. Most of them are frail and cold all the time."

"I hope the day never comes where I'd rather sit under an afghan and stare out the window than come down here and work with you." She gave Cassie's hand a squeeze and looked at her face. "What's bothering you, dear? You have a far away look in your eye."

Should she talk about Daniel? Grams had always shared wisdom and been really helpful no matter what the topic, but Cassie didn't feel like talking about relationships right now. She'd settle for the other option instead. "This case has me baffled."

"What case?"

"The murder? In the old mansion?"

"Oh, the Howard girl. Yes, so heartrending. She was such a sweet girl."

Cassie placed both hands on the counter. "Wait! You *knew* her?"

"Not well, but she worked with my friend Martha at Boersley's."

"Do you remember anything about what happened? Please! Tell me everything."

Grams rolled her head side to side to stretch out her neck. "Let me see. That was when… 1967?"

"Sixty-eight."

"Right. I was… twenty-six and pregnant with Thomas. Your mother Sandra was three, so Michael would've been five, and Mary seven."

"Wow." Cassie let the thought of all those young kids marinate in her brain. Her grandmother was a trooper.

"Ha. I was busy in those days." Grams smiled, and her eyes sparkled at the memory. "But before kids, I worked at Boersley's with Martha."

"I never knew you worked there!"

"Oh, yes. For about five years. That's how Martha and I became so close. Marilyn started working there after I left."

Cassie tried to picture a young Grams in a Boersley's shirt working a cash register. "So, Martha and Marilyn became friends?"

"Somewhat. Martha was quite older than Marilyn, but they were close enough that Martha was quite distressed at Marilyn's sudden departure. She was especially upset because her last words to Marilyn hadn't been nice. They'd had an argument."

"About what?"

"I don't know. She never said."

"What else do you remember about what happened?"

"Only what Martha had shared. She'd said Marilyn and her husband hadn't been getting along. He worked a lot and was barely at home. One day, Marilyn didn't show up for work and never did again. I believe Martha had stopped by the house a few times, but no one would answer the door. It wasn't until later we all heard the rumours of how both Marilyn and Wayne had left."

"Except Marilyn didn't leave." Cassie frowned.

"No. Unfortunately, she didn't."

Pumpkin flopped onto her side and meowed, clearly disappointed with the lack of attention. Grams reached over and gave the cat's belly a rub.

"Did Martha know about Marilyn's affair?" Cassie

asked.

Grams' eyes widened. "There was an affair? Oh, dear. No, I don't think Martha knew. Not that she ever mentioned, anyhow. How do you know?"

"Wayne told Brent about it during his interview."

"Is he a suspect, then?"

"Kind of. But he seemed just as surprised as we were that Marilyn's body was in the attic. And quite distraught."

"Some liars are good at lying." Grams pursed her lips.

"I know, but my gut says he's telling the truth."

"And sometimes you need to trust the facts and the evidence."

"True. I should follow up with Brent. He hasn't mentioned what else he's found out about Wayne." Cassie leaned on the counter. "What about your friend Martha? I hate to ask, but could she have been lying? You said she'd argued with Marilyn. Is there any way she could be responsible for the death?"

"I don't think so." Grams scrunched her face. "She was a loving woman. I doubt she could have hurt anyone."

"Some liars are good at lying."

"Touché." Grams sighed. "Maybe she could've if she'd been pushed hard enough. Any of us could be, I suppose—if horrible circumstances aligned. And no one knew Marilyn had been murdered, so it's not as if we were thinking about evidence at the time. But what would Martha's motive have been?"

"Whatever they argued about, perhaps? You did say she never told you what it was about."

"Maybe."

"Is she still around? Would I be able to talk to Martha about it?"

"Afraid not. She passed many moons ago. But you know her daughter. Maybe she knows something."

"Who's her daughter?"

"Jean—she was here the other day when I came in. She's a bigger lady."

"Oh! You mean the one whose friend had purple hair?"

"Yes." Grams grinned. "I can give her a call if you like. See if she'll have you over for a visit. She lives in my building."

"That would be great. Thanks!" Cassie kissed Grams on the cheek. This may be the break she'd been waiting for.

Chapter 17

Cassie pulled her SUV into a visitor parking spot at the Hilltop Manor Apartment Complex. Grams had moved here a few years back when she'd sold Cassie her store and building, and put her home on the market. She was more fit than most of the elderly living in these apartments, but she claimed to enjoy the company and the drastic drop in requirements needed to care for a house.

Next to the three apartment buildings stood the Hilltop Manor itself. A long-term care facility for those needing round-the-clock care. Cassie dreaded the day Grams would have to transition to that phase of life. On the other hand, maybe she never would. She was as spry and fit and mentally stable as a fifty-year-old, despite her age of seventy-eight.

Cassie double-checked the note on her phone with Jean's apartment number and stepped out of her vehicle and into the frigid air. The wind chill had picked up significantly, and Cassie felt as if the air would freeze her cheeks within minutes. She scurried to the door, squeezing her scarf around her neck and face.

Inside the foyer, Cassie buzzed up to Jean's apartment to be let through the security door. After a short elevator ride to the third floor, Cassie found Jean waiting for her with the door open.

"Come in. Come in." Jean allowed Cassie to pass through the doorway. "Did you bring your lovely cat?"

"Pumpkin? Oh no. Not today. She'd freeze her whiskers off out there!"

"It is a cold one, isn't it? Let me take your coat, and I'll make you a nice cup of cocoa."

Cassie pulled her arms out of her coat sleeves. "That sounds great. Thank you so much!"

"My pleasure, dear."

Cassie giggled inwardly. Was it a requirement to call people 'dear' if you were over the age of sixty?

At Jean's invitation, Cassie sat on the flowered loveseat in the living room. The apartment's layout was the same as Grams', only in reverse, with a small kitchen and living room, and one bedroom off to the side. Cassie smiled as she noticed a couple of wooden signs, a tin star, a lantern, and a candle set, all previous purchases from Olde Crow Primitives.

"Here you go." Jean handed Cassie a white mug with a purple, crocheted cozy buttoned around it, and squeezed herself into a rocking chair, barely fitting between the arms.

"Thanks."

"It's nice of you to come and visit. I'm glad your grandmother, Dorothy, called."

Cassie gripped the warm mug with both hands. "Grams thought you might be able to help me."

"I'll do what I can."

"Are you aware of the goings-on at the mansion on Elm Street?"

"I heard there was a bit of a kerfuffle." Dorothy adjusted a pillow behind her back.

"Do you remember the people who used to live there? Wayne and Marilyn Howard?"

"Yes. Marilyn was friends with my mother."

"I'm sorry, but they found Marilyn's uh… body. Someone murdered her."

Jean's hand flew to her mouth. "Oh, my! That's horrible!"

"It is. And I'd love to help find justice for Marilyn."

"How awful. The poor woman." Jean shook her head. "But what can I possibly do to help?"

"Tell me about your mother Martha's friendship with Marilyn."

Jean dropped her hands to her lap. "Let's see. They worked together at Boersley's. Sometimes Marilyn would come to our house and have coffee with my mom. She was in her twenties, I think?"

"And how old were you?"

"I must have been about... fifteen? One day, Marilyn disappeared. My mother was quite upset about it. I remember because I had a school dance to go to, and she was too upset to finish sewing my dress. It was your grandmother, Dorothy, who finished it for me."

Cassie smiled. Of course, Grams had finished the dress. She was an ever-flowing fountain of giving. "Did your mom ever talk about why Marilyn left? Or why she was so upset?" And was she possibly upset because she killed her? Cassie bit her tongue as the thought whirled through her mind.

"Not at the time, but she brought it up some years later. Apparently, their last conversation was an argument, and Mom felt like Marilyn leaving was her fault."

"In what way?"

Jean leaned forward and lowered her voice. "Marilyn had been having an affair. She'd confided in my mother about the whole situation. Mom was really upset about it and scolded her for her behaviour. She insisted Marilyn confess her deeds to Wayne and threatened to do it herself if Marilyn didn't comply."

"Oh?" Cassie pondered the notion. That showed morals on Martha's part. Not a motive for murder—yet.

"They argued about it, quite severely," Jean continued. "Mom didn't answer Marilyn's calls for a few days and ignored her at work. Then all of a sudden, Marilyn was gone." Jean picked at a piece of lint on her sweater. "Rumours said Wayne and Marilyn had a huge argument themselves, and they both picked up and left each other. Mom figured Marilyn must have told him about the affair. Then, when he blew up, she had nowhere to turn since Mom had been angry with her, too. So, she left."

"And your mom blamed herself."

Jean nodded. "I tried telling her it wasn't her fault, but she lived with the guilt the rest of her life. I'm glad she didn't know about the murder. She likely would've felt responsible for that, too."

"She's not the one who had the affair or committed the murder." As much as Cassie hated to admit it. There went another potential suspect. Unless her guilt was really about something else?

"No, but their friendship was important to Marilyn, and Mom knew it. She felt like she'd turned away when Marilyn had needed her most."

Cassie took a sip of the hot chocolate and licked the remnants off her lips.

"Who was Marilyn having the affair with, Jean?"

"I don't know. And as far as I know, Mom didn't know either. I don't think Marilyn ever told her."

"It would make sense. After your mom's reaction to the initial confession, Marilyn was probably on the defence."

Jean nodded. "I imagine that's true."

"Is there anything else you can think of that might be helpful?"

"I don't think so. But if I remember something else, I'll pop into the store."

Cassie stood. "Thank you. I'd really appreciate it. And thank you for the hot chocolate." She downed the last sip and carried the cup into the kitchen.

"Any time, dear." Jean rocked forward for momentum to get up from the rocker. "Don't be a stranger now!"

"I won't." Cassie slipped on her boots and winter outerwear.

"I'm sorry I couldn't be of more help."

"You were plenty helpful," Cassie said, even though that wasn't entirely true. She did appreciate the time the woman had taken to share her memories.

But as far as the case went, she was right back at square one.

Chapter 18

Cassie hugged herself as she sat in the SUV and waited for the windows to defog. Even though she hadn't been gone too long, the cold had taken hold of the vehicle all over again. She was glad she didn't have far to go.

Jean had been helpful in sharing everything she'd remembered about her mom and Marilyn, but it wasn't enough.

Sure, Cassie was fairly certain Jean's mom, Martha, wasn't the murderer, but she had never really settled on the idea in the first place.

She just didn't know where else to turn.

And she still didn't know the identity of the man Marilyn had an affair with. If she could find out, and the man was still alive, perhaps he could direct Cassie to the murderer.

Cassie shook her head. None of this made sense. The only person with an actual motive at this point was Wayne. Who else would want to kill a young, lonely woman who worked at a grocery store?

On the other hand, if Marilyn had confided in Martha about the affair, maybe she also confessed other secrets. Maybe there were motives no one else knew about yet.

But for now, there were none. None that had come to light through interviews, conversations, house searches, or evidence.

None.

Was it possible Wayne was a good actor, as Grams had suggested? Did he really murder his own wife?

Cassie refused to believe that. She'd seen the man learn of his wife's death, and that was not a man who held the guilt and weight of murder on his shoulders.

Did he?

This case was so frustrating. Would there ever be true justice for Marilyn?

The window finally cleared as the SUV warmed. Cassie pulled onto the street and headed up Main toward home.

A parking spot along the curb in front of Drummond's Bakery beckoned. Cassie pulled in. Even though her building was right across the street, the parking lot was around back. She didn't want to add any extra walking in the cold than necessary.

She hopped out and entered Drummond's. A couple of doughnuts would hit the spot right now and maybe even offer a little consoling. She should probably order something healthy for dinner instead, but she didn't feel like it.

Cassie took her place in line. Laughter pulled her attention to a group of men sitting at the corner table, dressed in firemen's pants and suspenders. She gulped and felt the blood drain from her face.

Spencer.

He ran his hand through his shoulder-length locks to push them away from his face as he laughed at the man across from him. His bicep bulged from beneath the edge of his navy T-shirt sleeve, and his eyes sparkled—until they met Cassie's.

Across the shop, they held each other's gaze until he broke contact, stood up, and told his friends he'd be back in a moment.

Cassie gulped as Spencer approached. Only a couple of months ago, he had professed his love for her. Then she'd ripped his heart out and stomped on it.

"Hey, Cassie." He ran his hand through his hair again.

She caught a whiff of his citrus shampoo, and her stomach churned. "Hi."

"How are you doing?"

"I'm okay. You?" They'd only talked once since the break-up, and that was when he stopped by her apartment to pick up a few things he'd left there. It was quick, and the conversation terse.

"I'm good. Yeah, good." He turned back to his table. "Just doing a little training with the guys today."

Cassie nodded. She opened her mouth to speak again but shut it when she realized she had nothing to say. Or at least nothing she could bring herself to say.

"Things at the store are good?" Spencer nodded to her building across the street.

"Yes."

"And you and Daniel? That's good?"

"We're friends. Nothing more."

Spencer's eyebrows briefly shot up but then returned to place. "I see."

Cassie swallowed again and moved up in line. "Spencer... I'm... sorry. Really sorry about what happened."

He waved his hand. "Nah. Don't sweat it. God had other plans." He looked over Cassie's shoulder, and his face glowed—like it used to when he saw her.

Cassie turned to see a young brunette woman, bound in a cute, red ski jacket, enter Drummond's. She made a beeline for Spencer and gave him a quick kiss on the lips.

"Hi!" She squeaked.

"Hey." He winked at her and put his arm around her shoulders. "Stephanie, this is Cassie. Cassie, Stephanie."

Cassie gulped and extended her hand. "Hi."

"Nice to meet you, Cassie." Stephanie shook it with a firm grip.

Spencer eyed his new girlfriend. "Cassie is the woman I was dating over Christmas before I met you."

"Oh." Stephanie nodded in understanding. "You own the primitive store. That's where I've seen you." She smiled.

"Yes," Cassie said, wondering what else Spencer had told this woman about her.

"I love your store. I've gotten lots of gifts for people there."

Cassie forced a smile, fighting the mixture of emotions jabbing at her heart. "Thanks. That's good to hear."

"Ready to sit?" Spencer gently rubbed the back of Stephanie's coat.

"Sure." She fluttered her eyelashes. Clearly, she was smitten.

And so was Spencer.

"Take care, Cassie." He smiled at her and gave her a quick nod.

"You, too."

He escorted Stephanie over to the other firefighters and grabbed a chair for her from the next table. She scooched close to him and nuzzled against his side, never giving Cassie a second glance.

Cassie turned her attention back to the line. She was next, and she was glad. The tears had already started to blur her vision, and she wanted to get home as soon as possible.

"What can I get you?" The lanky cashier adjusted his cap.

"Half a dozen doughnuts, please. Mixed."

Chapter 19

Cassie curled up on the couch under her favourite afghan with Pumpkin at her feet, doughnuts at hand, and a tissue box within reach. Already, a few wet, crumpled tissues sat on the coffee table.

Her emotions were at an all-time high, swirling around in an unending vortex in her mind. Spencer. Daniel. The murder. Spencer. Daniel. The murder. The pattern repeated itself over and over. Why couldn't she get it to stop? A fresh wave of tears rushed down her cheeks.

A light knock on the apartment door helped focus her thoughts.

Lexy let herself in. "Hey! How's it going?" She set a pizza from Wood Oven Pizzeria on the kitchen table and proceeded to squirm out of her winter gear. When Cassie didn't answer, Lexy looked over and immediately rushed to Cassie's side.

"What happened? What's wrong?" She plopped onto the sofa, causing Pumpkin to meow in disapproval.

Cassie sniffed and shrugged.

Lexy gently grabbed Cassie's shoulders. "Talk to me. What's going on?"

"I saw Spencer."

"Okay. And?"

Cassie swallowed to combat her dry mouth. "He has a new girlfriend." She sobbed again.

"Oh, honey!" Lexy pulled her friend into a hug. Then she let go and sat back. "It's never easy to see your ex with someone new, is it?

Cassie shrugged again.

"Talk to me." Lexy grabbed a chocolate doughnut out of the box. "What are you feeling?"

"I... I don't really know."

"Are you jealous?"

Cassie shook her head.

"Were you sad to see him happy with someone else?"

Cassie thought a moment and shook her head again.

Lexy furrowed her brows. "I'm not sure I understand what you're so upset about. Do you want him back?"

"Definitely not."

"So…"

"I don't know, Lex." Cassie let more tears stream down her face. "I don't understand it myself."

"Are you sure you don't still have feelings for Spencer?"

"I'm sure."

Lexy took a big bite of the doughnut and stared at the coffee table. After she chewed and swallowed, she turned back to Cassie. "What's his new girlfriend like? Do we know her?"

"I've never seen her before. But she's cute. Brunette. Obviously smitten with him."

"Yeah? And what about him? Did it look like he returned those feelings?"

"Very much so." Cassie picked at a loose string on her afghan. "When I tried to apologize to him for everything that had happened, he just shrugged and said it was fine. God had other plans."

"All right. Let's look at this from a different angle. Did it feel good to apologize to him?"

Cassie nodded. "I guess so."

"So, that chapter feels officially closed now?"

"It was already, at least I thought so."

Lexy shook her head. "No, it wasn't. You still carried around loads of guilt about hurting Spencer. But now you've seen he's not hurt anymore." She took another bite of her doughnut.

Cassie shrugged and continued to pick at the blanket.

"Cassie?" Lexy pointed her finger and jabbed her friend's knee.

"What?"

"How do you feel about Daniel, now?"

Another tear slipped from Cassie's eye. "The same. Why?"

"Because now you don't have an excuse. There's no reason not to be with him."

Cassie gulped. "What do you mean?"

Lexy grabbed a tissue and wiped chocolate crumbs from her fingers. "Your excuses for not being with Daniel no longer exist. You're not feeling sad at all. You're feeling fear. You have to face the truth. Do you want to be with him? Or don't you? It's time to decide."

Cassie buried her face in her hands. "No. That's not it."

"Are you sure?"

Cassie let out a low groan. "No. Maybe you're right."

"C'mon, girl!" Lexy slapped Cassie's leg and stood. "Time to face the music and admit the truth to yourself. Take a chance. Jump in—with both feet. No more tiptoeing around."

Cassie's heart skipped a beat. Was Lexy right? The vortex in her mind began to slow. There was truth in Lexy's words. She wasn't feeling sadness or despair. She wasn't jealous about Spencer, nor was she pining for him in any way. Could it really be all about Daniel? And facing her own fears?

Lexy used a clean tissue to grab all of Cassie's dirty ones. "We better start cleaning up."

"Why?" Cassie closed the almost empty box of doughnuts.

"It's almost seven. Everyone will be here soon."

"Oh! Bible study! I forgot all about it!"

"Why am I not surprised?" Lexy brought the dirty tissues to the kitchen garbage. "I'm going to put an alarm on your phone."

"Not a bad idea." Cassie tugged the corner of the afghan from underneath Pumpkin, who objected with a low meow. She ignored the cat, folded the afghan, and hung it across the back of the sofa.

"I'll do the rest." Lexy opened a cupboard and pulled out a few coffee cups. "You go take care of that red face of yours."

Cassie felt her cheeks. They were warm and raw. She went into the bathroom, splashed water onto her face, and gently dried it with a soft towel. She'd have to redo her makeup.

As she entered her bedroom, Pumpkin pushed her way in as well. After a few starting attempts, she jumped up onto the bed, flopped down onto the quilt, and thumped her tail against it.

Cassie took a moment to pet the cat and then drove her face into Pumpkin's warm, soft fur. After a few moments, Cassie turned her head and spotted her Bible on the nightstand. She reached for it and flipped it open.

It opened to Proverbs chapter three. Not a surprise, really. Cassie often read her favourite verses from that chapter, and the page had a crease in it.

Her eyes followed the highlighted verses on the page. Instead of reciting them, she thought deeply about their meaning. She wasn't supposed to lean on her own understanding. It wasn't up to her to figure things out. Her job was to acknowledge God in all things—to lean on Him. To trust Him. If she did that, He would direct her paths. He would show her the way to go.

"Oh, God," Cassie prayed. "I'm so sorry for trying to figure out this whole Daniel thing on my own. I got so scared after I messed things up with Spencer! But You're such a forgiving, merciful God. I know that in my heart, but I couldn't bring myself to believe it. I forgive myself for my mistakes, as You have already done. I ask You to forgive me for not coming to You with all of this sooner. You know the plans you have for me. And for Daniel. You know if we're to be together or not—if our relationship would bless you. I leave it in Your hands. Forgive me for ever trying to figure it out without You."

A quietness entered Cassie's spirit. She closed her eyes and let peace flow through her body. His peace. She rested in the stillness, then found herself humming a worship song about leaving it all at the foot of the cross. Her humming turned to singing, and she softly worshipped her Saviour in song.

Pumpkin snuggled up to Cassie's thigh and purred

loudly. Cassie continued to pray, "Lord, I ask you now to direct my paths. Show me Your plans. Not just about Daniel, but about anything and everything. What would You have me do next? I want to honour You with every ounce of my being."

Cassie continued to close her eyes and listen to her Lord. There was silence, but it was peaceful and restful. And then, the soft words spoke to her heart. She heard them as clearly as she could hear Pumpkin's purring.

Cassie's heartbeat sped up. Three simple words.

And finally, she knew what she had to do.

She glanced at her alarm clock. It was almost time for Bible study. Any moment, a wonderful group of women would gather in Cassie's living room to study the Word of God and pray together. They would delve into the meaning of the different verses and talk about applying them to their lives. They would discuss what actions they could take to use their lives to bring God glory.

Cassie jumped off the bed to redo her makeup. She'd never felt more excited about hosting Bible study. God was near because she had drawn near to Him.

And she couldn't wait to spend more time with Him.

Chapter 20

Cassie stacked the last few mugs in the dishwasher and set it to run, the rhythmic hum of the machine took over the kitchen.

Bible study night had been fabulous. The women dug into the book of 1st John, discussing how God is light. Cassie felt the Holy Spirit's presence with them as they prayed for ways to show God's light to others in Banford—and around the world.

Cassie placed the last few couch cushions in their place and collapsed onto the sofa.

"Rowr?" Pumpkin jumped up beside her.

Cassie checked the clock on the wall. Ten-thirty. "Ready to call it a night, kitty? I've got a good book I want to finish."

The cat rubbed her head against Cassie's leg and purred.

"Oh!" Cassie's hand flew to her mouth. "I forgot to send the candle order in after work!" She jumped to her feet, shoved on her fuzzy slippers, and grabbed her keys from a hook by the door.

"Meow?" Pumpkin chased after her.

"No, you stay here. I'll only be a—"

The second Cassie opened the door, Pumpkin bolted into the hallway.

"Or… you can come with me." Cassie giggled and then tittered again at the thumping noises her *fluffy* cat made as she bounced down the stairs in the quiet of the night.

Pumpkin waited for Cassie in the hall outside the door to Olde Crow Primitives. Cassie slipped the key into the lock and turned it until it clicked. This time, Pumpkin waited for Cassie to open the door and turn on the light before bounding in after her.

Cassie rummaged through the papers on the cash counter until she found the order form she'd written out earlier in the afternoon. She snatched it up and returned to the back door. She would use her laptop upstairs to enter the order, rather than staying here and using the bulky store computer.

"C'mon, Pumpkin!"

The cat followed her out the door and waited while Cassie locked it and pocketed the key. But when Cassie turned around, Pumpkin had disappeared.

Scratch. Scratch. Scratch.

"Stop that!" Cassie scolded the cat, who'd found her way to Daniel's bookstore door.

A faint light glowed underneath the door. Was Daniel there? It was so late.

Cassie gave a quiet knock and tried the knob. It clicked open. She let herself in, aware Pumpkin had already pushed past her leg and traipsed in like she owned the place.

Soft instrumental worship music played over the speakers. As was usual after hours, the mini-lights were lit, and the main lights dimmed. The hurricane lamps flickered in the windowsills, and the scent of mocha filled the air. Daniel sat on the area rug in front of the fireplace, chairs pushed back, and paperwork spread out around him.

Pumpkin ran to Daniel and headbutted his leg.

"Hey, you!" He looked up and found Cassie's eyes. "And you. What are you doing down here so late?"

"I could ask you the same thing." She smiled and approached.

"Taxes." He rubbed the back of his neck, his bicep pulsing beneath the arm of his T-shirt. "I have a meeting with my accountant next week, and I'm way behind with getting things prepared."

"Can I help?"

"Not really, but I welcome the break." He pushed aside two stacks of paper to make room for Cassie to sit beside him on the rug.

She sat, the warmth of the fire and of Daniel's closeness, almost making her dizzy. "We just finished Bible study, and I popped downstairs to grab an order I need to place before bed. Pumpkin noticed your light was on."

"Good kitty." Daniel scratched the cat's head.

Cassie grinned. "More like a destructive beast. She scratched the doorframe again."

"Maybe I should put in a cat door."

"Rowr?" Pumpkin's ears perked up. Both Daniel and Cassie laughed.

"So, how's the case going?" Daniel pushed more paperwork aside and stretched his legs out in front of him.

"Ugh. It's not. Nothing seems to make sense or fit together."

"Maybe I'll get you one of those big whiteboards for Valentine's Day. I hear they're all the rave at police stations and with the FBI."

"A whiteboard? How romantic." Cassie giggled.

"For now, I'll be your whiteboard. Talk to me. Tell me everything you know so far and who all the suspects are."

Cassie sighed. "It won't take long. Marilyn Howard worked at Boersley's Grocery. She'd been married to Wayne for three years but was mostly by herself at the mansion because he was often gone for work. She ended up having an affair. Her friend Martha at the

172

grocery store knew about it and reprimanded her. Martha insisted Marilyn tell Wayne about the affair, or Martha would do it herself. They had a huge argument."

"Wow. I didn't know that part."

"Yeah. I talked to Martha's daughter. Marilyn did tell Wayne, and then they both took off—or so everyone thought. Martha blamed herself for Marilyn's departure. She felt guilty until the day she died."

"That's so sad." Daniel pulled his knees up and rested his arms on them.

"Wayne had intended to return, but he never did. And as I said, everyone thought Marilyn had also left, but instead, someone murdered her and tried to make it look like she hung herself."

Daniel sighed. "Okay, who are the suspects?"

She held her index finger out. "One, Wayne Howard. He claims he didn't do it, and I want to believe him. My gut says he's innocent, and he looked completely shocked when he found out about the murder."

"But it *could* still be him."

Cassie nodded and moved to her next finger. "Two, Martha. Perhaps they had a fight about something else, and Martha really felt guilty about the murder, not Marilyn leaving."

"And what does your gut say?"

"That it's not her, either. But I can't just rely on my gut. I need to look at the facts."

Daniel reached out and touched Cassie's arm. "But

your instinct is usually spot on. I don't think you can ignore it completely. Who else do you have?"

"Well, I kind of suspected Edward Morris for a time."

"Anna's grumpy neighbour?"

Cassie nodded. "Yes."

"Why did you stop suspecting him?"

"I don't know, really. I kind of... forgot about him. I think I only figured it might be him because he's so miserable and doesn't like people."

"Well, maybe it *was* him. Who was Marilyn having the affair with?"

"We don't know. We..." Cassie's eyes widened, and her mouth fell agape. "Wait! Do you think she could've had the affair with *Edward?*"

Daniel raised a brow. "It's possible. Actually, that makes a lot of sense. He would've been young back then. He lived across the street. When did he marry?"

"I'm not sure. But I could find out."

"If he's a suspect, then what about Charles? The other neighbour?"

Cassie shook her head. "No. I forgot to list this in my evidence before, but the ghost is a factor. Someone is trying to scare people away from the house. They did it before, likely to keep people from finding the body, and they did it again this week. The house had also been completely ransacked because someone searched for something. Charles wouldn't be capable of those things in his state. His dementia has progressed too far. Nor would he have been able to elude me—or Brent—when we searched the house.

"Okay." Daniel scratched his head. "Then Edward it is."

Cassie smiled. "I think you're right. Yay!" She lunged forward to hug Daniel.

He almost fell backward with her enthusiasm but managed to maintain his balance as he wrapped his arms around her.

Cassie held on longer than she'd intended to. He smelled like mocha and leather. His muscles rippled under her fingers, and she was sure her heart skipped about three beats. Slowly, she let go and leaned back.

"Now that I know how you'll react, I'll be sure to be much more helpful in the future." Daniel winked, his eyes glistening in the firelight.

Cassie felt the heat rise to her cheeks. She folded her legs to her side and stroked Pumpkin's tail. "I, uh… saw Spencer today."

"Oh?" Daniel ran his hand over the back of his neck.

"He's seeing someone new."

"Really?"

"Yup." Cassie avoided Daniel's gaze. "So, I guess three out of three people are all okay after my slip up in dating him last year."

"Looks like."

"And Lexy came over before Bible study. We talked things out a bit."

Daniel stretched his legs out and leaned back onto his hands. "Good. How do you feel?"

"Like I have no excuses left." She took a peek at Daniel's face but quickly lowered her eyes again. "And then I spent some time with God, sorting things out, confessing sin, asking for forgiveness, worshipping…"

Daniel continued to watch her and wait. Patiently.

"And, um…" Cassie swallowed. "God spoke to me."

"Oh? What'd He say?"

Cassie met Daniel's eyes again, this time keeping them steady on his. "He told me to… go to you."

Daniel's eyes flickered, and his mouth twitched. "So… what do you plan to do about that?"

Cassie inched forward, bringing her leg to the point where it touched Daniel's. "I don't know. What do *you* think I should do?" She smirked.

He lifted one hand off the rug and cupped her face. "You know what I think." Daniel's eyes gazed deep into her soul and held her in a trance.

Cassie lingered in the moment, wanting it to last as long as possible.

Daniel caressed her cheek. "I love you, Cassie Bridgestone. I've loved you from the moment I first laid eyes on you."

Cassie gulped and surprised herself when a tear slid down her cheek. "Thank you for waiting for me," she whispered.

"You're worth the wait." Daniel moved his hand

around the back of her head and pulled her toward him.

Cassie leaned in, their lips almost about to touch. But she hesitated and rested her forehead against his. "I love you too, Daniel."

And then he closed the gap. His lips grazed hers, and she could taste a trace of the mocha. Then he pulled her in even closer, pressing his lips tightly on hers.

All the electricity she'd ever felt from Daniel's touches manifested into huge lightning bolts shooting up and down her spine. Her arms tingled, her legs felt numb.

Their lips lingered on one another's for a minute before they parted. Daniel's arms enveloped Cassie in a full embrace, and he held her tightly against him. His muscles pulsed against her back. She drank in his scent with a new fervour.

"Rowr?" Pumpkin rubbed up against both Daniel and Cassie.

"Looks like she approves." Cassie smiled.

"Good kitty." Daniel patted the cat on the head. Then he returned his hand to Cassie and stroked her hair. "So… will you go to dinner with me on Valentine's Day?"

"That depends. Where would you be taking me?"

Daniel leaned back quickly, causing Cassie to collapse in a fit of giggles.

Chapter 21

"Rowr?" Pumpkin pushed her nose against Cassie's face, gently rousing her from her deep sleep.

"Pumpkin? What are you doing?" Cassie glanced at her alarm clock. "It's too early to get up."

Knock, knock.

The cat pushed against Cassie again.

"What…?"

Someone was at the door.

Cassie groaned and pulled herself out from under the cozy quilts. She straightened her flannel pyjama pants and top. It was her new favourite winter set, covered in cartoon cats holding coffee mugs.

Knock, knock, knock.

"Coming!" Cassie mumbled, redoing her messy

bun. She yawned and opened the door.

"Good morning!" Daniel swept into the apartment, grabbed Cassie around the waist, and twirled her around.

She leaned her head on his chest to fight the dizziness. "Not. A. Morning. Person. Remember?"

Daniel squeezed her and kissed her forehead. "I'm sorry. I couldn't wait to see you." His eyes lit up, and a grin stretched from ear to ear. His muscles filled out his tight sweater nicely, and his hair was neatly gelled and styled.

Cassie smiled, despite her weariness. Then she looked down at her attire and wrapped her arms around herself in a self-conscious hug. "Ugh. I look awful! Let me go change."

"No way," Daniel flicked her messy bun. "You look absolutely adorable."

Cassie shrugged. Maybe love really was blind.

"You sit with Pumpkin on the sofa, and I'm going to make you a Daniel Sawyer breakfast special." He directed her to the living room area.

Cassie snuck off to brush her teeth and returned to sit on the sofa and watch Daniel, humming as he pulled pans from the cupboard, eggs and bacon from the fridge. He clicked the stove on and had the food sizzling within minutes.

Daniel poked his head back into the fridge. "Do you have any mushrooms?"

"No. Sorry. Can I help?"

"Nope." He held his palm up. "You stay there and take time to wake up. I'll make a tea for you."

"I could get used to this." Cassie giggled. Pumpkin jumped up to the back of the couch, and Cassie rubbed the cat's lower back.

Daniel, holding the fridge open with one hand, turned to face her. His eyes sparkled. "This is only the beginning."

Chills ran up and down Cassie's spine. She silently thanked God for Daniel and praised Him for his goodness and mercy. After the previous night's kiss, Daniel and Cassie chatted until almost two in the morning. When she got home, she fell into the most deep, peaceful sleep she'd had in ages. Even with only a few hours of slumber, Cassie felt rested, and her heart felt full.

Twenty minutes later, Daniel brought two full plates and two small juices to the coffee table on a tray.

"This looks amazing!" Cassie admired the artistry in which Daniel had placed the eggs, bacon, and toast on her plate. He'd even cut her toast into the shape of a heart. "You're so sweet!"

He kissed her forehead again. "Anything for you."

Cassie pulled the plate onto her lap and dug her fork in the egg to break the yolk.

"Wait," Daniel said. He grabbed her hand. "Let's pray first. I want to keep God first in everything we do."

Cassie's heart melted at his words. He had been *so* worth the wait. A hundred times over. "Of course."

Daniel took the lead and prayed thanks to God for His goodness, for sending His Son Jesus, and for the food. Daniel also thanked God for bringing him and Cassie together in perfect timing.

Butterflies flittered around Cassie's stomach, taking away her appetite. But she ate anyway. And when they finished, she snuggled next to Daniel, pulling her legs up and leaning against his side. She delighted at how well they fit together.

Daniel traced his finger up and down her arm. "I'd like to find some kind of couple's devotional we can read together every day. Would that be okay?"

"I love that idea."

"Perfect. I have one or two in the bookshop, but I'm not sure they're the best ones. Maybe you can come take a look later? See what you think?"

Cassie smiled at his enthusiasm. "Sure."

"I have something else." Daniel sat forward so quickly that Cassie fell over. Was this to be a regular occurrence? "Sorry. But stay here. I'll be right back."

Cassie sat up again and watched Daniel disappear into the building hallway. A few seconds later, he returned, holding a giant, thin rectangle wrapped in brown paper.

"What is that?" Cassie leaned over the back of the couch, carefully studying the package as Daniel brought it closer. It had to be some sort of painting.

"It's your Valentine's Day present."

"What? You're a few days early!"

"I know, I know. But I couldn't wait any longer. I've been dying to give this to you!" Daniel plopped down beside her and slid the package across the floor until it sat in front of her.

Cassie tried to keep the heat from filling her cheeks, but she was sure she failed. But, her embarrassment quickly turned to excitement the second she pulled at the brown wrapping. As she tore it away, she gasped at the wonder in front of her.

It was a DJ Sawyer black-and-white photograph of two eagles on the ice.

"This is beautiful!"

"I'm so glad you like it! It took me a few trips to the blind to get the perfect shot."

Cassie examined the exquisite feathering on the eagle. "It looks like you took this from five feet away."

"Well, I *am* a professional…"

Cassie giggled and leaned the framed photograph against the coffee table. She wrapped her arms around Daniel. "Thank you! I love it."

"And I love you."

Cassie's cheeks instantly heated as she stared into his eyes.

Daniel grinned. "And you better get used to hearing it because I'm going to tell you all the time."

His lips beckoned her. Should she kiss him? Her heart raced, and her palms turned sweaty. This was all so new with Daniel. And exciting.

Before she could decide, he answered her question.

He touched his lips to hers in a soft, slow kiss.

Cassie's nervousness fled in an instant. Having her lips against his seemed the most natural thing in the world.

Daniel pulled back first. "I wish I could do this all day. Stay here with you, and hold you in my arms. But I have to run. I'm hoping to get a couple more hours of tax paperwork done before opening."

Cassie smiled. "That's okay. We'll see each other later."

"You can bet on it." He kissed her forehead and stood, grabbing the dishes from the coffee table and stacking them onto the tray.

"Please—leave those." Cassie reached out and touched his arm. "Let me do it."

He pulled her to her feet and wrapped his arms around her again. "Thank you."

"Thank *you*. You're the one who made me breakfast and brought me a beautiful gift."

Daniel placed his hand on the back of her head and held Cassie as she nuzzled into his chest. "You're welcome."

They finally let go of each other, and Daniel moved toward the door. "Do you have anything special planned for today?"

"Well…" Cassie, hands behind her, leaned back against the kitchen table. "I plan on visiting the mansion before work to check out a hunch based on last night's conversation."

"Cassie—"

"Don't worry. I'm going to text Lexy and have her and Brent meet me there."

Daniel's shoulders relaxed. "Promise?"

"Yes."

He stepped up and gave her a quick peck on the lips. "Be careful. And be sure to pop in the bookstore and tell me all about it when you get back."

"I will." She waved as he winked and walked out the door.

Hopefully, she would have something to tell.

Chapter 22

Standing on the sidewalk in front of the old mansion, Cassie shoved her mittened hands into her coat pocket and hunched her shoulders to keep her collar bunched around her neck. The wind chill dropped the already below freezing temperatures another few degrees, making the biting air almost unbearable.

Lexy and Brent should've been here by now. Cassie turned her gaze to Zach and Anna's house across the street. Zach had already left for work—should she stop in and see Anna, to warm up a little? No. That probably wasn't a good option. Anna had been feeling rather sluggish the past few days, and Cassie didn't want to take the chance she'd wake her friend if she was still sleeping.

Another gust of wind sent a needling sensation through Cassie's cheeks. She was going to freeze if she stood out here any longer. She eyed the covered porch and shuffled up the snowy walkway, opting to seek cover from the icy blasts.

Unfortunately, the shaky porch roof did little to deter the winds coming from all sides. What was taking Brent and Lexy so long? Another freezing swirl of wind and snow whizzed by her face, this time making her eyes water and freezing the tears onto her eyelashes.

Cassie sighed. She should've driven her SUV. At least then, she could've been sitting in a warm vehicle.

But she had chosen to walk, and she couldn't take the freezing Canadian temperatures any longer. Cassie jiggled the front door handle and sighed in relief when the door popped open. The mansion was still very cold inside, but at least it would provide shelter from the wind. She would just stay by the front door until Lexy and Brent arrived.

Cassie's phone vibrated. Lexy texted that someone had come into the station to report a snowblower theft. Brent was finishing up the paperwork. Cassie sighed. Hopefully they wouldn't be long.

Time ticked by as Cassie analyzed the room, looking for ways to test her theory. Since her last visit, the investigative unit had returned and thoroughly searched the house, looking for evidence pointing to the murderer. *Something* in this house was being sought after, but the team had neglected to find it. In their wake, they'd left piles of books, papers, and files, beside emptied bookshelves, cabinets, and the piano bench.

Where else could she look? Cassie pulled out her phone to check the time. Lexy and Brent still hadn't arrived, and she'd have to open Olde Crow Primitives soon.

There was no time to waste.

Cassie turned on her flashlight, and moved about the room, ignoring the piles and debris. Instead, she focussed on the empty cabinets and shelving, examining each for thin seams or moving parts.

There hadn't been any secret passages in the house, but it didn't mean there weren't secret compartments. And there *had* to be. Cassie counted on it.

After a thorough examination of all the furniture, baseboards and paintings in the living room, Cassie moved to the dining room and then the kitchen. She opened all the cabinets and ran her fingers along all the edges but found nothing but dust and fifty-year-old grime.

A search of the other rooms downstairs also proved to be futile. Cassie then found herself standing at the base of the grand staircase. She looked around. The ruthless wind sought crevices to force its way inside the old mansion. Was it safe to go upstairs before Brent and Lexy arrived? Cassie shrugged. She'd already made her way around the entire main floor. Surely if someone was here, they'd have shown themselves by now. And Brent and Lexy would unquestionably show up any minute.

Cassie's mission dominated her thoughts. She carefully made her way up the stairs, examining each riser and tread for movement or false fronts.

Again, nothing.

Cassie groaned as she reached the second floor. She *had* to be right. She just had to be. There was no denying the earnestness of her hunch.

She entered a bedroom. The mattress was still on its side like the last time she'd been here. The old metal bed frame and springs left no possible place for a secret compartment.

She stepped up to the wardrobe. The clothes had been stacked in a pile on the floor beside the massive wood structure. She opened the large doors to find a few mothballs rolling around in the bottom. The sides were merely thin panels, with no space for anything to be hidden.

Cassie aimed her flashlight at the top. The curly, wood design had been glued on. Again, no space for anything extra.

She tried the bottom. A thin panel across the foot of the wardrobe shifted a little. Cassie's heart sped up. She rocked the panel back and forth until it came loose. When she pulled it away, a hole appeared, with only the floorboards showing beyond it—nothing else.

Cassie sat on the floor and sighed. So close!

Suddenly remembering her shortage of time, she rose and moved on to the dresser in the corner. If she searched the whole house and found nothing, she could wallow about it later. But for now, she needed to make the most of every minute.

Like everywhere else, the dresser contents had been emptied and stacked in piles on the floor beside. There was no sense going through them, as they clearly had already been searched. Cassie pulled out the top drawer, completely removing it. She flipped it over to check the bottom. Finding nothing, she ran her hand across the inside of the dresser to check for space at the top.

Not wanting to spend a lot of time on one piece of furniture, Cassie quickly removed all the drawers. No doubt the investigative team had already checked the bottom of each, so it was wasting time for her to do it again. What she was looking for wouldn't have been taped to the bottom of any drawer.

Cassie scanned the floorboards and the baseboards as she had downstairs, but everything seemed solid, so she moved on to the next bedroom.

This was the bedroom with the old bookshelf. Cassie gasped. The old books were scattered across the floor. She picked up an open, weathered copy of *The Secret Garden* with bent pages. Obviously, the books were damaged anyway due to the home's neglect, but the investigation team's careless treatment of them made her stomach turn.

Despite the pressure from lack of time, Cassie took a moment to stack the books neatly and push them to the side.

The bookcase had been pulled away from the wall, but a quick glance told her nothing was behind it. She looked at it from the front again.

There were five shelves, but something was odd about the middle one. Cassie studied it a moment and smiled as she realized the difference.

The back wall of that particular shelf protruded out more than the others.

She quickly ran her fingers along the odd piece. It looked like a false backing. Cassie picked at the edges with her fingernails, trying to pull it loose. When that didn't work, she pushed along the top edge and then the bottom.

When her fingers reached the side edge, her push caused the other side to pop forward, like a lever.

Cassie's heart sped up again as she reached behind the open space and pulled the board loose. As it gave way, a dusty, leather-clad book fell out.

A diary.

She knew it! Cassie resisted the urge to squeal out loud as she grabbed the journal and carefully unwound the leather strap holding it closed.

The first page told her everything she wanted to know—Marilyn's name, followed by a start date of January 1966 and a hyphen with no end date listed.

This is what the killer had been looking for.

This was the proof! Within its pages, Cassie would find all the answers to the looming questions. Who the affair was with, and more importantly, who killed

Marilyn Howard.

Brent would be relieved when he saw the diary.

Speaking of Brent, why wasn't he here yet? And where was Lexy?

Cassie flipped through the journal's brittle pages, careful not to rip apart ones that were stuck together. The ink had faded, but with the help of her flashlight, Cassie could make out the gist of the writing.

Marilyn was lonely. Entry after entry mentioned how she missed Wayne and how marriage wasn't what she'd thought it would be. Some entries talked about Marilyn's garden, and a few about her friend Martha at Boersley's, but nothing too interesting.

Cassie couldn't wait. She quickly turned to the back of the journal, skipping past the blank pages until she came to the last few entries, looking for Edward's name. She glanced over Marilyn's details about a fight with Martha and how Martha had threatened to tell Wayne about the affair. The story more or less divulged the same details Martha's daughter, Jean, had shared.

Cassie flipped back a few pages.

An entry caught her eye.

Marilyn mentioned something about an underground tunnel. How she'd gone to meet *him,* but he insisted she didn't use the tunnel as she was too precious to walk through something so gritty.

So, there *was* a secret passage. But where? How? Under the road? And where did it start?

Cassie flipped another page back.

Marilyn detailed how Wayne was gone for another business weekend, and she was glad. It would give her time to spend with her true love, the one who treasured every moment with her.

Another page back.

This entry was about a girl at work fighting with her parents. The previous entry about having to eat dinner with Wayne while pretending she still loved him.

But so far, no evidence leading to Marilyn's killer.

Cassie flipped to the next page back.

Marilyn outlined a romantic, candlelit dinner with her one and only love. She detailed the roasted chicken she'd cooked and the salad she'd prepared with greens from her own garden. Cassie blushed at a few details outlining an after-dinner rendezvous, and then how—

What?

Marilyn wrote how *Charles* had spent the night with her here at the mansion.

Charles? From next door?

So, he *had* been the one Marilyn had the affair with?

But then who was the murderer? Who had searched the house and caused the ghostly impersonations? Charles wasn't capable of it, so who else had a motive?

Not Edward. He was obviously cleared as a suspect now. So, who?

Cassie's eyes widened.

Wayne. It had to be Wayne. Grams had been right. He was a good liar. He was the only one with a motive. Jealousy had won him over and caused him to do the unthinkable.

Cassie gripped the diary. She'd have to read through every page. Somewhere in this book was the proof showing Wayne was the culprit. There had to be, or else he wouldn't have been so determined to find it.

A floorboard creaked out in the hall.

"Brent?" Cassie called. "Lexy? I'm in here! I found Marilyn's diary! It'll tell us all we need to know."

A figure in the doorway caused a shadow to fall over the already weak light in the room. Cassie looked up.

Charles loomed over her. "Thank you, Miss Bridgestone. I'll take that."

He held out a hand, waiting for her to pass him the diary.

In his other hand, he held a gun.

Chapter 23

"Charles!" Cassie exclaimed as she placed the diary on the floor and slowly stood while lifting her arms until her hands were in the air.

Charles waved the gun around. "I told you to hand me the diary, not to place it on the floor." His cheeks were red from the cold, and a navy toque covered his bald head. The hand holding the gun shook.

"Of course." Cassie, careful to not make any sudden movements, bent her knees at a snail's pace and lowered her hand to pick up the diary. "I've got it right here."

Charles snatched the diary out of Cassie's hand and pointed the gun at her. His eyes darted to the door and back to Cassie.

"You don't have to do this, Charles."

His bottom lip quivered. "I don't have a choice."

"We always have a choice." Cassie took a slow breath. "And we can always make the right choice."

Charles hunched a shoulder and brushed his cheek against it. "I don't know *what* to do."

"How about we start with you handing me the gun?" Cassie slowly reached her hand out.

"No! That's not helping. Stand back!"

"Okay, okay. Sorry."

Charles paced in front of the door, occasionally glancing at the diary in his left hand.

Cassie silently prayed for courage and wisdom. She suddenly realized Charles hadn't repeated himself or done anything remotely similar to someone who had dementia. Other than the fact he was obviously distraught at the situation, his mind seemed coherent with no lapse in lucidity.

"You remembered my name," Cassie said.

"Of course, I did." He sighed. "And I remember your friend, Anna, too."

"You faked dementia?"

"It was all I could come up with at the time. And obviously, it worked."

Cassie thought it despicable anyone would fake such a horrible disease. But then, apparently, Charles was also a murderer. In light of that, it wasn't such a stretch.

She'd have to come at things from a different angle.

"I only peeked through the diary, but from what I read, Marilyn was deeply in love with you."

He stopped and looked at Cassie, his eyes hollow. "And I loved her. With all my heart."

"What happened then, Charles? Tell me about Marilyn."

Tears welled up in his eyes. With a careful grip on the diary, he wiped the tears on the back of his glove. "She was... exquisite." He leaned against the doorframe and stared at the wall, his mind evidently drifting off to another time and place. "Wayne, her husband, was gone all the time. He worked long hours in the city and spent many weekends on business trips. She was alone and lonely. I used to watch her through my window, puttering around her garden for hours. No one so beautiful should be treated that way by their spouse."

Charles lowered the gun and pointed it toward the floor. "One day, she showed up at my door. A light bulb had burned out, and even with the aid of a small ladder, she couldn't reach it. I went over without hesitation to help. She repaid me with homemade cookies. We ate them while enjoying a cup of coffee and light conversation. After that, she frequently appeared at my door with requests. I fixed a loose shutter, set a mousetrap, killed a spider, took out the heavy trash. Task after task turned into daily visits, and before I knew it, I discovered I'd fallen in love."

Cassie waited for Charles to go on, but he continued staring off into space.

"That's understandable," she said. "Did she reciprocate those feelings? How did the affair start?"

Charles gulped. "One day, I was on the ladder trying to fix an upper kitchen cabinet door. When I came down, I missed the last step and fell. Marilyn tried to catch me, and we somehow ended up in each other's arms. I knew I shouldn't have, but I kissed her. I couldn't help myself. But she gladly returned the kiss and came back for more."

"And then?"

"We couldn't get enough of each other, but we had to be careful. One day, while I helped her clean out the crawl space in the basement, we came across a tunnel. It led to the garden shed in the back yard, next to my property line. I placed my shed next to it and connected them with a door between. With the flowers planted along the property line in front of the sheds, no one noticed. I started using the tunnel to sneak over to see Marilyn, out of the way of neighbour's prying eyes."

"Like Edward's." Cassie nodded.

"Yes. He hasn't changed."

"Did he ever find out about the affair?"

Charles shook his head. "I don't think so. Once things became serious between Marilyn and me, we took every precaution to keep our love hidden."

"And this tunnel, is this how you escaped the house after you threw the vase at me?"

"I'm sorry about that. I only meant to scare you. The vase wasn't supposed to come so close to hitting you. And yes, I went to the attic when you came in, and came back down to the second floor to warn you off. I snuck downstairs when you went outside to wait for Brent and went home via the tunnel. Parts of it had crumbled over the years, but I still managed to get all the way through to the shed, where I waited until everyone left."

Cassie pondered this new bit of information, relieved to finally have an answer to the elusion but still unclear about the murder. "Tell me about Wayne discovering the affair."

Charles sighed. "We did our best to keep everything on the down-low, but one day Marilyn decided to confide in a friend at the grocery store."

"Martha."

"Yes. She didn't tell Martha who I was, but it couldn't be hard for her to figure it out if she tried. Regardless, Martha surprised Marilyn by getting angry and threatening to tell Wayne."

"Which she did." Cassie shifted her weight to one leg. "And Wayne got upset."

"He did. He left. And then I…"

"You what, Charles? What did you do?"

"I didn't mean to…" He dropped the diary and the gun to the floor and buried his face in his hands. "I loved her. I really loved her."

Cassie stepped up to Charles, kicked the gun away, and gently rubbed his arm. "It was an accident?"

He nodded and squeaked words out between sobs,

"I loved her. After she talked to Martha about us, and then told Wayne, I was furious. I yelled at her that I didn't blame Wayne for leaving. She slapped me, and…" He sobbed again. "I… I pushed her away. She fell and hit her head on the edge of the first stair. It was horrible. There was blood all over. I held her but… she wouldn't answer me. And then she just stopped breathing."

The sobs came heavily now, and Cassie pulled Charles into a full hug. It didn't matter that he'd held a gun to her only moments ago. This man wasn't a real killer at heart. He needed compassion and forgiveness. Like everyone does for one sin or another.

"I was horrified." Charles stepped back from Cassie's hug. "She was the love of my life and…"

"It was clearly an accident," Cassie said. "But you felt you had to hide it?"

Charles nodded. "I cleaned her up and put a headband in her hair to cover the wound. I dressed her in her favourite dress—the one she often wore for me when we had our romantic dinners—and brought her to the attic. I made it look like… Oh! It was so horrid what I did!"

"But if people thought she committed suicide, it would let you off the hook."

"Yes. At least I thought it would. I didn't know at the time that suicide victims automatically had autopsies performed on them. They would've figured out it was murder."

Cassie pressed on. "But no one found the body."

"No one. I thought for sure Wayne would come back, but he never did. In fact, no one ever showed up—ever. Days turned into months, and then years. Every day I looked out my window at this big house, thinking about my love hanging in the attic, all alone. And no one knew."

A moment of silence followed before Cassie decided to see what else Charles would tell her. "Why did you fake the hauntings?"

"Kids started coming around the mansion after it had been left for so long. I had to do something to keep them out. I had to protect Marilyn and the house. But I couldn't bring myself to go inside. I placed a speaker in the upstairs window and ran the wire behind the drainpipe and through the grass to my yard. It seemed to do the trick. The kids still busted some windows with rocks, but for the most part, they stayed away."

Cassie sighed in understanding. "And you boarded up the broken windows?"

"I had to do something. I couldn't let the house die with her, but after so many years of Canadian winters, there wasn't any more I could do. Not without going inside or investing a lot of money."

"And then we came along and changed everything."

Charles wrung his hands. "I had no choice but to come back into this house. Marilyn had told me she'd kept a diary about us. I couldn't let the police find it and tie me to the murder. Except my searches came up empty."

"And you tried to scare us away."

"It was a lazy attempt, but I didn't know what else to try. Even though it was awful setting foot in here again. The memories came flooding back with a force I didn't expect."

Cassie rubbed his arm. "You must have had a difficult life, living with all these consequences."

Another tear slipped down his cheek. "Yes. And it's about time I set things right and let Marilyn go in peace."

"Cassie! Cassie!" Brent appeared in the doorway with Lexy at his side. "Stop right there!" He yelled at Charles.

"Easy! Easy!" Cassie held out her arm. "It's okay. He's not going to hurt me."

Brent looked from Cassie to Charles. "What's going on here?"

"Charles is who you've been looking for," Cassie answered. "He told me everything. That diary on the floor is Marilyn's, and it tells all about their relationship."

"I thought you had dementia." Lexy stared at him.

Charles merely shrugged.

Brent noticed the gun on the floor by the window. He rushed over to it and snatched it up. "What's this? Did he try to hurt you, Cassie?"

"No. I'm fine. And he's ready to turn himself in, right Charles?"

"Yes." Charles stared at the floor. "Yes, I am."

Brent gently put the old man's arms behind his back and snapped on a set of handcuffs. As he ushered Charles out of the room, Brent glanced at Cassie. "Why didn't you wait for us? You promised me you wouldn't come in here by yourself! Once again, you put yourself in unnecessary danger!"

"I'm sorry. I knew you were coming, and I only had a bit of time."

"Still no excuse." He stared Cassie down. "You should've waited for us."

The seriousness of the situation suddenly dawned on Cassie. Lexy and Brent *hadn't* been there yet. And Charles *had* had a gun pointed at her. What would've happened if—

"I'm glad you're okay." Lexy hugged her. "And you solved the case!"

"Yes, there is that." Brent guided Charles to the stairs. "Thankfully."

"You're welcome." Cassie tried to smile, but couldn't. One woman murdered, and two men's lives upturned in the process. Both stayed single the rest of their lives, refusing to try and love again, and both lived with heavy guilt from their sinful choices, not to mention Marilyn's.

It was sad, but at least now the chapter had closed.

Chapter 24

"It's a perfect day for this!" Daniel trudged through the snow ahead of Cassie, following the river path on the way to the bird blind. The sun beamed down on Banford, keeping the temperature just above freezing. The low wind chill factor added to the warmth.

"It is. In more ways than one." Cassie adjusted her backpack, weighted with all her birding equipment. Charles had given Brent a full confession, and, in light of his age and the circumstances surrounding Marilyn's death, was expected to receive a reasonable sentence. Marilyn could finally be put to rest.

Cassie studied Daniel as he plodded along the path ahead of her. So much had happened this week! Not only was another murder solved, but her jumbled love life had finally fallen into place. She was with the man she loved—a man who loved God more than her, and her more than himself. And in return, Cassie felt the same way. God was first, then Daniel and then herself. It was the order God intended. God was good, and it was Cassie's pleasure to honour Him with every bit of her and Daniel's relationship.

Her phone dinged in her pocket.

She checked the text and squealed. "Anna had her baby! It's a boy!"

Daniel turned back and gave Cassie a hug. "That's great news!"

Cassie leaned in to share a quick kiss, the action sending shock waves through her body all over again.

They walked on, and as they came to a corner in the path, the shrubbery opened up offering a clear view of the water. Far out at the ice's edge, a light mist hovered over an open section of water. A sequence of quick screes drew Cassie's attention upward.

"Look!" Cassie pointed. A pair of eagles circled high in the sky.

Daniel turned to her and joined Cassie at the water's edge to watch.

The eagles danced around each other, soaring higher and higher. Cassie wanted to pull her binoculars out of her backpack, but she couldn't take her eyes off the courting pair, even for a second.

The eagles parted, then flew together again, coming together in a well-measured connection.

Then their talons locked.

"Oh!" Cassie squealed. "Do you see it? Do you see

it?" She jumped up and down and latched onto Daniel's arm.

"I do." He put his hand over hers.

And the eagles plummeted to the earth, swirling around and around, cartwheeling at an intense speed toward the river.

Neither Cassie nor Daniel made any move toward their cameras or other equipment, their eyes steadfast on the phenomenal display before them. No device could enhance this moment.

The raptors spiralled downward, only seconds from the ice before they released their grip of each other and flew to safety.

Cassie's heart thudded in her chest, and her mouth hung agape. She and Daniel continued to stare out at the ice where the eagles had been moments before.

"Marry me." Daniel voiced the words with a sheer determination that stole her breath.

"What?" Cassie swung her gaze to the handsome, Godly man beside her. "What did you just say?"

Daniel's sparkling eyes met Cassie's as he turned to face her. "Marry me, Cassie. Be my wife. My forever companion."

Cassie's mouth hung open again. Was this real?

He took both her hands in his. "I mean it. I love you. I know it's early on, and it might seem crazy, but I've never been more certain of anything in my life other than God. And I know He's the one who's brought us together."

Cassie gulped. "Say it again." Her eyes welled up with tears.

Daniel continued to hold her hands as he knelt on one knee in the snow. "Will you marry me, Cassie Bridgestone?"

Cassie nodded as the tears escaped and fell down her face. "Yes! Absolutely!"

Daniel leapt to his feet and pulled Cassie into a tight embrace.

Cassie squealed and kicked her feet up behind her while Daniel held her above the ground. Then he gently let her down and found her lips with his own.

And then they sealed the deal.

***

Cassie sat across from Daniel at a private table at Hardcastle Pub and Restaurant. The place was full for Valentine's Day, but Daniel had managed to pull some strings and secured a secluded corner table for their romantic dinner.

Lexy and Brent sat on the opposite side of the restaurant, enjoying their own dinner. The couples had exchanged hellos on the way in, but other than that they kept to themselves to celebrate Valentine's Day.

The fire roared in the nearby fireplace, and the candlelit centrepiece flickered on their table. Daniel met Cassie's outstretched hand in the middle of the table and interlaced it with his own. The diamond ring on her finger sparkled in the candlelight. They'd gone to the jewellers earlier in the day to pick it out. Sometimes it all still seemed surreal. She was engaged! To Daniel!

He grinned, shadows flickering across his face enhancing his rugged jawline. "I have one more gift for you."

"Another one?" Cassie couldn't help but smile, but felt a little guilty she'd only gotten him a bird book and a chain with a cross on it—even though he'd loved both gifts.

"You better get used to it. I plan to spoil you for the rest of your life."

"Only if you let me spoil you, too."

Daniel let go of her hand, reached into the inside pocket of his suit jacket, and pulled out a small velvet jewelry box.

"What's this?" Cassie let him place the box in her hand. "More jewelry? I'm quite happy with this." She waved her hand in the air to draw attention to her ring.

"Just open it." He grinned.

Cassie flipped the top open. A shiny key was fastened to the inside with a red ribbon. "What's this for?" She furrowed her brows. "I already have a key to your apartment. I'm your landlord. And I don't think this is quite approp—"

"It's not to my apartment."

Cassie tilted her head and studied Daniel's grinning face. "Then what…"

"It's to a house."

She furrowed her brows again, trying to make sense of everything. "You're moving out of the apartment?"

"Silly!" Daniel grabbed Cassie's hand and squeezed it. "It's to *your* house. *Our* house. On Elm Street."

Cassie gasped, and her free hand flew to her mouth. "You bought the mansion?"

"You said you loved it, right? I thought we could give it the love story it deserves. Together, after we marry."

Tears streamed down Cassie's cheeks. Did he really? "How... how did..."

"I talked with Wayne. After everything that happened, he had no problem parting with it."

"But it's so run down. How will we ever...?"

Daniel smiled and took her other hand, so he held both in his own. "I've already spoken with a couple of different construction crews who specialize in restoring historic buildings."

Cassie blinked a few times. "But the cost..."

He snickered. "I'm DJ Sawyer, remember? You don't have to worry about the cost. All you need to do is pick out your preferences and tell the crew. They'll make it look however you want."

"Oh, Daniel!" Cassie sniffed.

"I love you, Cassie Bridgestone. And I can't wait to begin our life together."

"I love you, too." She smiled at him. "And I can't wait, either."

DID YOU ENJOY THE BOOK?

Could you spare a minute and please leave an online REVIEW for *Faith, Rope, and Love* at Amazon, Goodreads, and BookBub? It's the best thing you can do for an author, next to buying the book. Thanks!

DO YOU WANT MORE?

Guess what? There's a SECRET VAULT with more of Banford! Sign up at <u>wendyheuvel.com</u> to become a member of the Tea with Wendy club. You'll also receive my newsletter. You'll get access to:

❀ A FREE BANFORD SHORT MYSTERY

❀ A DETAILED MAP OF BANFORD

❀ FLOOR PLANS OF CASSIE'S BUILDING (stores, apartments)

❀ PHOTOS

❀ PUZZLES & GAMES

❀ RECIPES

❀ WEEKLY UPDATES, GOD MOMENTS, AND MORE PHOTOS

Enter the SECRET VAULT at <u>wendyheuvel.com</u> today for the exclusive content.

READ OTHER BOOKS BY WENDY HEUVEL:

ABOUT THE AUTHOR

 WENDY HEUVEL solved the Rubik's Cube when she was eight, but now can't remember why she went into the next room. Canadian by birth, Dutch by blood, and British by heart, she resides on 26 acres with her husband, kids (Things 1, 2, 3, &4), three floofy kitties, and monster dog. She's passionate about Christian mission work, travelling, birding, and eating potatoes.

Sign up for *Tea with Wendy* newsletter for freebies, book news, access to the secret vault, special gifts and promotions: www.wendyheuvel.com

FOLLOW WENDY:

 wendyheuvelauthor

 @wendyheuvelauthor

 Wendy Heuvel

 Wendy Heuvel

Wendy Heuvel

wendyheuvel.com

Made in the USA
Middletown, DE
11 August 2023

36533762R00135